Secret of the
Super-small
Superstar

Also by Lin Oliver

WHO SHRUNK DANIEL FUNK?

BOOK 4

Secret of the Super-small Superstar

Written by Lin Oliver
Illustrated by Stephen Gilpin

Simon & Schuster Books for Young Readers
New York   London   Toronto   Sydney

For the Wolf pack—Cole, Nicky, John, Thomas, and Spencer—for showing me the best about boyz and friendship—L. O.

For Nemo, the big little brother—S. G.

SIMON & SCHUSTER BOOKS FOR YOUNG READERS
An imprint of Simon & Schuster Children's Publishing Division
1230 Avenue of the Americas, New York, New York 10020

SIMON & SCHUSTER BOOKS FOR YOUNG READERS is a trademark of Simon & Schuster, Inc.
For information about special discounts for bulk purchases, please contact Simon & Schuster Special Sales at 1-866-506-1949 or business@simonandschuster.com.
The Simon & Schuster Speakers Bureau can bring authors to your live event. For more information or to book an event, contact the Simon & Schuster Speakers Bureau at 1-866-248-3049 or visit our website at www.simonspeakers.com.
Book design by Tom Daly based on an original design by Lucy Ruth Cummins
The text for this book is set in Minister.
The illustrations for this book are rendered in ink.
Manufactured in the United States of America
0810 FFG
10 9 8 7 6 5 4 3 2 1

Library of Congress Cataloging-in-Publication Data
Oliver, Lin.
Secret of the super-small superstar / by Lin Oliver ; illustrated by Stephen Gilpin. — 1st ed.
p. cm. — (Who shrunk Daniel Funk ; bk. 4)
Summary: When an eagle gets stuck in the Hollywood sign, it unexpectedly results in Daniel's family learning about his ability to shrink, and meeting his toe-sized twin, Pablo.
ISBN 978-1-4169-0963-7 (hardcover)
[1. Size—Fiction. 2. Twins—Fiction. 3. Brothers—Fiction. 4. Bald eagle—Fiction. 5. Eagles—Fiction. 6. Family life—California—Los Angeles—Fiction. 7. Los Angeles (Calif.)—Fiction. 8. Humorous stories.] I. Gilpin, Stephen, ill. II. Title.
PZ7.O476Se 2010
[Fic]—dc22
2009040012
ISBN 978-1-4169-9906-5 (eBook)

ACKNOWLEDGMENTS

Hey, hey, hey. Not so fast, dudes. So you thought you could skip this, huh? Well, no such luck. I say you have to read on because this is the place where I say thanks to all the GUPs who have helped make this book. And let's face it, saying thanks is important. Oh, don't pretend like this is a newsflash or anything—I'll bet your mom or dad has pointed this out to you once or twice, or maybe, like, even a million times. So here goes. I'm going to say a totally huge thank you to Navah Wolfe, for being a humongous help and an eagle expert to boot, and to David Gale, for being an everything expert and a most cool editor. Way to go, team. And hats off to Ellen Goldsmith-Vein and all the Gotham folks who are fabuloso. And of course, hugs and fist bumps to my SCBWI office mates—Steve, Kim, Sara, Aaron, GeeCee, Sally, and Brandon—for being the best of the best and making the tree house such a great place to be creative. Love hanging with you, dudes. And to the Baker boys (hey, you know who you are: Alan, Theo, Oliver, and Cole), like Clint says, you guys make my day.

—The Funkster

Just because Daniel's bigger than me, doesn't mean he gets to hog all the thanks. So, yo, thanks from me too.

—The Pablo

THE CAST OF CHARACTERS

DANIEL

PABLO

LARK

VU

GREAT GRANNY NANNY

THE CAST OF CHARACTERS

GOLDIE

ROBIN

MOM

GRANDMA LOLA

PRINCESS

Hey, it's me. And I'm back with another rip-snorting, rootin'-tootin', gut-splitting, crowd-pleasing prologue.

Originally, I had decided not to start this book with a prologue at all because between you and me, I was feeling pretty prologued out. I mean, I've already written three prologues for my other books and I ask you, how many good prologues does a guy have in him? Not too many, I can tell you that.

But you're in luck, because at the last minute, I changed my mind and decided to write one anyway. Why? Two very important reasons.

The first is that you guys asked for it. Well, maybe not *all* of you. But I think one guy did. His name is Dixon Dorkoff, and he lives in Omaha, Nebraska. He wrote me a letter saying, "Dan, your last prologue was the funniest prologue I've ever read. It was also the *only* one I've ever read." How can you say no to a compliment like that? The poor guy was practically begging me. So, Dixon, here it is. This prologue is for you, dude. Lap it up.

The second reason I'm writing this is that, believe

it or not, I actually have something important to say. And the subject is keeping secrets.

Now, I'm not talking about the kind of ridiculous secrets my sisters are always trying to keep, like what color dress they're wearing to the Spring Fling or who likes who in fourth-period English, or if some girl they don't even know is meeting a ninth-grade boy at the mall. Girl secrets are so weak. Once, my sister Robin actually cried for an entire day when one of her friends let the word leak out that Robin thought Ryan Howe's dimples were really, really cute. Give me a break, folks. Everyone knows Ryan Howe's dimples are cute. I mean, they're right there on his face, big as craters on the moon.

No, that is definitely not the kind of secret I'm talking about keeping. I'm talking about *big* secrets, life-and-death ones. In my case, that's the kind of secret I've been asked to keep, and let me tell you, it's hard. Not just hard, but *super* hard.

A little background, just for grins.

I think you already know that about a month ago, I discovered I have an identical twin brother named Pablo who is the size of the fourth toe on my left foot. (If you don't know that, dudes, you have some serious reading to catch up on!) I came across him totally by accident when I shrank to the size of a toe too.

According to my Great Granny Nanny, this shrinking thing runs in our family. But it's a big secret, and she says we can't tell anyone. I can't even tell my mom. I mean, she doesn't have a clue that I can make myself shrink by giccuping (a giccup, for you guys who are not into digestion sounds, is a kind of watery disgusto burp) and make myself unshrink by sneezing. This is not an easy secret to keep, especially from my mom who has been tracking my body sounds since I was a baby. Okay, I know that sounds weird, but when you think about it, it's not. I mean, the woman changed my diapers and taught me to poop on the potty, for gosh sakes.

Granny says no one can know about Pablo, either. She says if scientists found out about him, they would lock him up in a laboratory cage and poke him and prod him and study his every move. Pablo would hate that. That little guy loves freedom so much, he can't even sleep with his feet tucked in at night. He would definitely not make it in a cage.

So now you get the picture. I am the keeper of not *one* but *two* life-and-death secrets. Sometimes I feel as if they're just going to come popping out of me like that annoying jack-in-the-box my little sister Goldie used to play with nonstop (until I decided it had to be buried in my underwear drawer so she couldn't find it). I get worried that one day, I'll just open my mouth and—bamo-slamo—blurt out the truth. So far, I've resisted the temptation to blurt.

Until last Saturday, that is.

That's the day Pablo and I got discovered by Hollywood. Now, that might sound like a great thing to you, but for me, it was a very dangerous thing, and here's why. If there's one thing I know about being a star in Hollywood, it's that *everyone* wants to know *everything* about you. You can't have any secrets. I mean, think about your favorite stars. I'll bet you know a ton about them . . . their favorite band, the name of their first pet, whether they wear boxers or briefs, what they do with their toenail clippings, if they're a popcorn type or an M&M's type at the movies, how many encounters they've had with three-headed Martians. All that stuff.

Well, imagine if one of them happened to have a secret mini-brother and the ability to shrink, like me. Sooner or later, those little facts would be revealed. Everyone would find out, which in my case, would mean that my secrets wouldn't be secret any more. The world would know about Pablo. And about my shrinking tendencies. And that would spell big-time trouble for both of us.

But on the other hand, the promise of fame was sure tempting. I'd be rich. I'd be powerful. Everyone in the world would know my name.

Which, by the way, is Daniel Funk. Yeah, that's me. Daniel Funk, world-famous superstar. Or not.

Read on to find out.

CHAPTER 1

The Funkster's Funky Fact #1: In the comic books, the very first vehicle Batman owned was not the Batmobile but a Batplane.

"Daniel!" my mom shouted, flinging open the door to my room with such force that it felt like a class-five hurricane had blown in. "I need you! This is an emergency!"

I was lying on my bed right there in front of her eyes. But because I had shrunk down to my toe-sized self, she didn't see me. It's a known fact that when you're under an inch tall, you don't attract a lot of eyeball attention.

It was last Saturday. Pablo and I had spent the morning playing one of our favorite games. We call it Curtain Crashers. What we do is climb up to the windowsill in my room and take turns jumping onto the curtain fringe. Then we pump really hard until we're swinging like mini-monkeys back and forth across the room. When we're as high as we can go, we holler out "Curtain Crashers!" and let go of the fringe, doing as many flips and turns as we can before coming in for a crash landing on my bed. It's

fun, because when you're that small, you can zip and zoom through the air like a half-crazed fly.

I had just finished my third jump of the day, a double twist featuring *both* a frontward and backward somersault, and was sprawled out on the pillow in the recovery position. Pablo was trampolining across the bed toward the windowsill to take his turn. At the sound of my mom's voice, he froze in his tracks.

"GUP alert, bro," he whispered.

GUP is Pablo speak for Grown-Up Person. Personally, I don't have anything against grown-ups, but my brother Pablo is not a fan of your average GUP.

"Dude! Hide yourself!" he commanded.

I didn't need to. One of the major advantages of being the size of a toe is that you can be smack-dab in front of your mom and not be seen. You have no idea how useful a thing that is. Like, if your mom is looking for someone to clear the table or take the trash out or worse yet, clean up the dog poop from the backyard, you are basically invisible.

Man, do I ever love that.

"Where is that boy?" my mom muttered as she marched around my room, shooting a suspicious glance at Stinky Sock Mountain. She actually stopped and gave it a little poke with her toe. *What was she thinking? That I'd be hiding in a pile of my own smelly socks? No way. I can handle one or two stinky socks, but lying around in a whole huge pile of them is definitely out of the question, even for me.*

She held her nose and left the room, calling, "Lark! Lola! Granny! Has anyone seen Daniel?"

"The coast is clear," Pablo whispered to me. "My turn."

He jumped onto the rope that hangs from the mini-blinds and climbed up until he reached the windowsill. I have to admit, I felt a little guilty about continuing our game. I mean, my mom *did* say it was an emergency.

"Oh, no, you don't," Pablo said, seeing me hesitate. "No quitting before I show you my new move—the Pablo Plunge. It's killer."

"But Pabs—"

"The Pablo is not listening. Now, are you ready to play, D. Funk?"

"Yeah, sure. Ready, P. Funk."

The thing about Pablo is, you can't say no to him. He's like a twenty-four-hour fun machine, and who can say no to that? Not me.

Pablo grabbed the curtain fringe and started to swing. His black cape was billowing out behind him and he looked like a teeny-weeny Batman as he sailed back and forth. Great Granny Nanny makes him these really cool capes out of my old action figure clothes, but Batman is his favorite. Pablo says he loves him best because he fights crime with his brain and not with a gun. I'm sure Granny Nanny taught him that. She's all for nonviolence.

"Lettin' go, bro!" Pablo shouted when he had reached launch height.

He let go of the curtain, stuck his chest out like he was doing a high dive, and flapped his arms like a mini-bird. I think he actually caught some air because he sailed up almost to the ceiling before he started his free fall.

"Curtain Crashers!" he hollered as he came careening headfirst toward the bed. "Taking the Pablo Plunge!"

He never made it to the bed, though. Midway through his descent, a hand reached out and caught him.

CHAPTER 2

The Funkster's Funky Fact #2: The average person has 550 hairs in each eyebrow.

Oh, don't worry. It wasn't the hand of an evil villain or Dr. Death or anything. Just the opposite, in fact. It was a little wrinkled hand with a peace symbol ring on the index finger. That ring was a dead giveaway. Without even looking up, I knew it was our Great Granny Nanny. She's always telling us that war is not the answer, peace is. In fact, she even has that on a bumper sticker plastered across the front of her mint green motor scooter.

"Listen here, hotshot," she said to Pablo. "This is not okay."

Granny Nanny scooped me up from the bed too, and plopped me in her palm next to Pablo. She put her face so

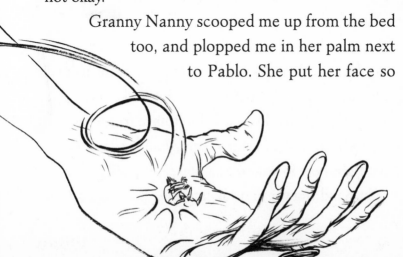

close to us that you could see the little gray flecks in her blue eyes. That was the good part. The bad part was that you could also see that one of her eyebrow hairs was really long and kind of crazy looking, like it had decided to separate from the others and go its own way. It's weird how you see every detail when you're little.

But let me just say, I really love Granny Nanny no matter how long her eyebrow hairs are.

"What's the problemo?" Pablo asked her.

"Didn't you hear your mother calling you?" she asked me. "She's frantic. Some kind of bird emergency."

"Sounds major," Pablo answered. "Somebody lose a tail feather?"

Pablo and I both cracked up. Granny usually thinks Pablo's jokes are funny, but this time, she didn't laugh. She took off her glasses and gave me a look.

"All I know is that your mother has been searching for you, Daniel. And if you don't want to make her suspicious, you better unshrink. Like now."

"But Granny, I can't. I don't have to sneeze."

"Which is why I keep a handy-dandy supply of pepper right here in your desk," she said, pulling open the right-hand drawer and taking out a little Santa Claus pepper shaker we used to put out at Christmas. We don't use it anymore because the Mrs. Claus salt shaker that went with it broke into a million pieces when I knocked it off the table by accident one year. (Hey, it wasn't my fault that someone left it on the very edge.)

Granny put me down on my bed, shook some pepper into her hand, and waved it under my nose.

"Breathe in, hotshot," she said. "This should do the trick."

Boy, did it ever! When I got a whiff of that pepper, my nose started to tingle and that made me want to . . .

"Ah . . . ah . . . ah . . . AH CHOOOOOOOOOOOOOOOOO!"

. . . sneeze. Before you could say Jolly Old Saint Nick, I had sprung back to my original,

AH-CHOO!

slightly-taller-than-average sixth-grade size. My head was spinning, which would happen to you, too, if you sprouted up four feet in less than a second.

"Was that you sneezing, Daniel?" my mom called out. I told you she was an expert on my body sounds.

She walked into my room and seemed surprised that I was there, and even more surprised that I was standing on my bed.

"What are you doing up there?" she asked.

"My feet were asleep, so I put them to bed," I blurted. You've got to admit, that was a pretty clever thing to say, under the circumstances. My mom, however, wasn't all that amused. She glanced over at Granny and gave her a *what's up with him?* kind of look.

"Boys," Granny said with a shrug. "They think they're such a hoot."

My mom looked suspicious. "I was just in here, Daniel," she said. "Where were you?"

"Uh . . . excellent question, Mom."

"Then how about an excellent answer."

I stood there on my bed with absolutely nothing in my head. Zippo. Empty. Lights on, nobody home. I think I had used up all my brainpower with that classic "putting my feet to bed" remark. So I just said the first thing that came to my mind.

LIN OLIVER

"I was . . . um . . . organizing my baseball cleats. In the closet."

My mom gave me a look that said *I'm not buying that, buddy.*

"You only have one pair of cleats," she pointed out.

"All the more reason to be very, very organized about them."

Okay, that was a pathetic answer, but I had already launched my story so I had to stick with it. I shot her a confident smile, like this was a normal conversation.

"The one thing a baseball player can't have is disorganized cleats," I said. "Ask any Dodger."

Lucky for me, this sorry excuse for an excuse was cut short when Lark, my fifteen-year-old sister and Queen of the Geeks, wandered into my room carrying her mini video camera that goes everywhere with her. She's always on the lookout for boring stuff that she can shoot to put on her boring video blog. That's her hobby, being boring.

"And this conversation," she said, pointing her camera at me and talking to her imaginary audience, "is just another example of how the male brain is inferior to the female brain."

Lark is the family expert on how boys stink and

girls rule. You can read her opinions on her blog I-Think-I-Know-It-All-But-Really-I'm-Just-A-Ding-Dong dot com, but I wouldn't recommend it unless you want your eyes to roll back in their sockets and never come out again.

Next, the Larkster pointed her camera at my floor, zooming in to capture a close-up of Underpants Valley, which, in case you're not familiar with the layout of my room, can be found just next to my blue leather La-Z-Boy chair which is next to Stinky Sock Mountain.

"Look at this pile of underwear, dear blogsters," she said. "You certainly won't find something like this in a female's room."

"That's because females don't wear boxer-briefs," I said, sticking my face so close to her camera that anyone who was unlucky enough to watch her video would be forced to look up my left nostril.

"Daniel, get your nostril out of my video," she complained.

"Wish I could, Lark, but I can't tell my nostril what to do. It has a mind of its own."

She was about to lunge for me when my mom stopped her.

"Kids! Stop this silliness!" she said. "I don't have time for this. We have to leave right away."

"But Mom, it's Saturday!" I protested. "My day to relax. Where do we have to go?"

"Daniel, have you forgotten already?" she answered. "Today is Robin's volleyball finals at John Burroughs High. She left early this morning for warm-up, and I told her we'd all be at the game by one o'clock."

Yup, I sure had forgotten. Robin, my fourteen-year-old sister who is a pretty satisfactory jock in a girly kind of way, had led her middle school volleyball team to victory in their playoff game a couple of days before and now they were in the championships. By the way, you should have seen her after

that playoff game. All she did was hug her team-mates and cry. You wouldn't believe the crying. I mean, it was waterworks city. If you ask me, and I know you didn't, I don't get why girls cry when they *win* a game. Seems to me, you should cry when you *lose* a game.

You'd think that living in a house with six females—a great granny, a grandma, a mom, and three sisters—I'd have gotten a clue by now about how they think. But I have to say, their womanly brains just don't make any sense to me. Like crying when you win a game. Or washing your hair every day. Or talking on the telephone when you don't have anything to say. Who thought those things up?

Girls, that's who.

"Come on, Daniel," my mom was saying. "Grab your things and let's go."

I checked out the race car clock in my room. It was only ten thirty, so I didn't see why she was in such a humongous rush. I was hoping to get in another few rounds of Curtain Crashers.

"Listen, Mom. I don't mean to be a party pooper, but we don't have to be at Robin's game for another two hours."

"That's two and a *half* hours, math genius," Lark pointed out.

In case you hadn't noticed, Lark is a major pointer-outer, which is only annoying twenty-four hours a day. That girl . . . oh, excuse me . . . that *woman* (don't ever call her a girl or she will freak out) will point out everything that's wrong with me at the drop of a hat, and you don't even have to ask her. No kidding. If she were sitting next to you right now, she'd just start pointing out all my faults . . . . that I have poor hand-washing skills, that I snort when I laugh, that I wear my T-shirts inside out, that I turn in messy homework, that I—

Wait! Now I'm doing it. Someone stop me before I turn into a pointer-outer, too!

My mom is really nice and hardly ever gets impatient, but by now, she was tapping her foot and jingling her car keys. That key-jingling thing is a sure sign she's dying to get going.

"Daniel, please hurry and put some shoes on," she said. "Lark, go get your sister Goldie and meet us at the car. I have an emergency call that I have to make before the game."

"What's the emergency?" I asked.

My mom is a vet, and it's not unusual for her to get called for emergencies that are pretty weird. Like the time this kid Marcus Waxman called crying because he had accidentally dropped his goldfish Sam in the toilet bowl. The kid was freaking out because Sam was hiding down at the bottom of the bowl and the fish net wasn't long enough to reach way down there and scoop him out. Don't worry, my mom rescued Sam before there was any flushing involved. Then there was another time she was called to untangle a pregnant guinea pig that got her foot stuck in her cage treadmill while she was actually giving birth to five little piggies. That was gnarly.

But if you think those were weird, they were nothing compared to the bird emergency my mom proceeded to tell us about.

"There's a bald eagle stuck in the Y of the Hollywood sign," she said, as though that was a sentence regular people just popped out every day.

"Probably just another bird trying to make it big in Hollywood," I said.

I heard a high-pitched laugh coming from the pocket of Granny's apron. I glanced down at it and saw Pablo's head poking out. Granny must have dropped him in there when my mom arrived, but knowing The Pabs, he was not about to stay put and be quiet.

"Sshhhh," Granny said to her apron pocket, before she could stop herself.

My mom looked confused.

LIN OLIVER

"To whom are you speaking, Granny?" she asked.

This required fast action on my part. I stepped in front of Granny and started to laugh really loudly to distract my mom. She was looking at Granny as though she had just flipped her wig.

"I bet that eagle came to Hollywood to try out for *American Idol*," I said. "He'll probably sing 'I Believe I Can Fly.' It's a big hit with the endangered-bird crowd."

I hooted really loud at my unfunny joke, and it worked. My mom forgot all about Granny talking to her pocket.

"Bald eagles are no longer endangered," she said to me, speaking in her vet voice. "They have been delisted, thank heavens. But that poor bird may be injured. There are some crazy people with shotguns who think it's cool to shoot at an animal."

My mom's cheeks got all blotchy and red at that thought, which is what happens when she gets really angry. I can always tell when I'm in trouble by the number of blotches on her cheeks.

"Don't even go there, Mom," I said. "I bet Mr. Eagle's just taking a rest from flying. Giving his wings a break."

"Or maybe he has a broken wing," she answered, her eyebrows bunching up in a worried look. "A fracture might easily destroy his flight capabilities."

I could see that my mom was really starting to panic. She is a major bird nut and she has this special thing for eagles, which is why she named me Daniel Eagle Funk. That's right . . . Daniel *Eagle* Funk. Laugh if you want to, but I'll bet there's a ton of you out there with strange middle names too. My cousin Nick used to tease me, until I pointed out that his middle name is Bebop. Don't ask me why, ask my Uncle Morris.

Anyway, I wanted to calm my mom down about the eagle and everything, so I said, "Don't worry. He probably just got off course while he was migrating. I bet he's fine."

But she wasn't about to be calmed down.

"Whatever the situation," she said, jingling her keys some more, "the Hollywood sign is an extremely poor habitat for any bird, let alone the *haliaeetus leucocephalus*. I have to go to him immediately."

Here's a tip, guys. When your mom starts throwing around long Latin names for delisted endangered bird species, do not try to argue with her. Trust me, it will get you nowhere. Just do what she says.

So I got my shoes, threw on a sweatshirt from the floor, checked into the bathroom for a quick pit stop (let me know if this is too much information), went outside, and climbed into our minivan.

My mom already had the motor running. Since I was the last one in, I had to sit in the way back with Granny Nanny. The front seat had my mom, her vet supplies including a cage for the eagle, my grandma Lola, and two trays of her freshly baked *yemarina yewotet dabo*, which, in case you're not up on your Ethiopian desserts, is a spiced honey bread. (What? You didn't know that? Then you obviously don't live with my Grandma Lola who teaches world culture and has never met a weird foreign food she didn't love.)

In the middle seat, there was Lark, her camera, her big mouth (which takes up a lot of room if you include all the hot air it blasts out), my little sister Goldie, and her Barbie doll who was dressed in a pink volleyball outfit with a snappy change of clothes for after the game. And in the way back, the seat that I swear is designed to make kids nauseous on road trips, were Granny Nanny and me.

If you're wondering where Pablo was, Granny Nanny had told him he couldn't come, which made him plenty mad. He complained that he never gets to go anywhere, but she told him there would be too many people in the gym and he was taking a chance on getting discovered.

As we pulled out of the driveway, I scrunched my

hand into the pocket of my sweatshirt to see if there were any leftover gummy bears that I could munch on during the ride to Hollywood.

You'll never guess what I found in there.

I'll give you a hint.

It was the size of a toe and was wearing a Batman cape.

CHAPTER 3

The Funkster's Funky Fact #3: Each letter in the world-famous Hollywood sign is fifty feet tall. (You can see a picture of it from space at www.hollywoodsign.org.)

It's about a thirty-minute drive from where we live in Venice, California, to the Hollywood sign, which is up in the hills above—yup, you guessed it—Hollywood. The whole way there, Lark was running her camera and her mouth, and I don't know which was more annoying. Okay, I do know. Her mouth. That girl was commenting on everything, and I mean *everything*, she was shooting from the car window.

"On my left, you'll see the freeway, crammed with cars of every color," she babbled.

I ask you, friends, why would anyone bother to point that out? I mean, what *else* would you expect to find on a freeway. Kangaroos?

"On my right, you'll see the other side of the freeway. Notice the busy, busy people, driving to and from work."

Did she say "busy, busy people"? Yes, she did. What were we . . . in kindergarten? I remember my teacher, Ms. McMurray, reading us *The Busy, Busy Bee* book about how the little critters are always busy, busy, busy making honey and such. It was boring even then, and I was only five. No, I definitely had no intention of sitting there listening to any busy, busy talk about bees or any other species. I had to speak up.

"It's Saturday, Larkster," I blurted out. "Most people are NOT busy, busy, busy because they don't work on Saturday."

"Barbie does," Goldie stated very matter-of-factly. "She and Ken work at Jack in the Box."

This is what I live with, folks. My sisters are all on a permanent vacation in la-la land.

"Hate to break it to you, Golds, but Barbie and Ken do not work at Jack in the Box."

"How do you know, Daniel? Did they tell you that?"

"Newsflash, Goldfinch. Barbie isn't real. And hold on to your hat, but neither is Ken."

Goldie stuck her tongue out at me, and I noticed that it still had some strands of shredded wheat on it. I forgave her for that, though. After all, she's only seven and a half, and a kid that age is entitled to have some leftover breakfast food hanging off her tongue. But this doll habit of hers had to end. I felt it was high time she dropped Barbie and picked up a *real* toy, like a lightsaber or a monster

LIN OLIVER

truck or a Brothers of Destruction action figure.

"Goldie, don't you think you're getting pretty old to be playing with dolls?" I asked, trying to be gentle. I really didn't want her bursting into tears because when she cries, her nose runs, and that creates snot which dribbles out of her nose and she refuses to wipe it off and . . . well, I think you get the picture why making her cry was not an option.

"Daniel," Lola said, turning around from the front seat to make her point. "In many native tribes, people worship spirit dolls their whole lives. I myself enjoy the presence of my Winged Cloud Dancer doll while chanting in my sweat lodge."

"I like dolls too," Granny Nanny chimed in. "Back in the day, I dated a wrestler named Muscles Malone, and he was what I'd call a *real* doll. Va-voom!"

Welcome to my world, dudes. Spirit dolls and sweat lodges and Muscles Malone are just normal freeway talk for the Funk family. Enough said.

I reached into my pocket to see how Pablo was doing. At first, I couldn't find him, so I stuck my index finger deep into the corner . . . you know, where the lint from the dryer clumps up in little gray wads. Sometimes when he's hanging out in Granny's apron pocket, Pablo takes a nap and makes a pillow from those wads. I gently poked the first lint ball I encountered. A little voice called out.

"Yo, up there. Do I poke you when you're trying to catch some z's?"

No one else in the car could really hear Pablo, because from a distance, his voice sounds like a squeaky mouse. Even though my ears have gotten pretty good at making out his words, I knew I needed to shut him up before anyone else noticed the squeaking.

"Pipe down," I whispered, opening my pocket so he could hear me. "You aren't supposed to be here."

I thought I could sneak that little warning in without catching anyone's attention. My mom was deep in thought about the bald eagle, Lola had begun doing some spontaneous chanting, Goldie was totally involved in making a Barbie ponytail, and Lark was hanging out the window annoying people with her camera.

But wouldn't you know it, big ears Lark did notice.

"Of course I'm supposed to be here, Daniel," she said. "I'm covering Robin's game for the school website. I even have a special pass that allows me to interview the players afterward."

She reached into her pocket and pulled out a

cheesy plastic badge on which she had written, "Lark Sparrow Funk, Official Press Pass."

Ordinarily, I would have pointed out to her that anyone who is even remotely normal is not interested in anything a bunch of sobbing girl volleyball players have to say before, during, or after a game . . . but since I wanted the ride to be quiet and peaceful, I bit my tongue and didn't say a word. Well, I did say a word. Actually seven words. And they were:

"Nice badge, champ. You make it yourself?"

I know, I know. It wasn't exactly the kindest

remark, but give me a break, folks. Some opportunities a guy just can't pass up.

Finally we reached the Hollywood sign. Seeing it was a major thrill. Those nine letters spelling out H-O-L-L-Y-W-O-O-D are way bigger than you think. When you look at the sign in the movies, or even in real life from Hollywood Boulevard, it looks pretty normal size, for a sign, that is. But when you're up close, you see that each letter is as tall as a five-story building. They're just sitting there on the scruffy brown mountaintop looking all famous and everything.

Man, oh, man, I hope you get there one day, because it's some sight.

We drove up a street called Beachwood Canyon, which dead-ends at the Hollywood sign. There's a gate you have to go through to walk up to the actual sign, which is kept locked most of the time. There were two cars and a truck parked in front of it.

"You the bird nut?" a man in a ranger uniform asked my mom as she turned off our car engine.

"I am a veterinarian specializing in bird life," she answered. As you know, my mom is a real fan of the entire bird species, and she's pretty fussy about how people refer to her beloved feathery friends.

"I'll take you up there," the man said. "Looks like that crazy eagle's got himself stuck in the Y. Don't suppose you know why he chose the *Y* over the *H* or the *D* or any of the other letters?"

"No," my mom said with a smile. "We didn't cover that in vet school."

She's nice to everyone, my mom. I remember my dad telling me once that he thought she was the sweetest person he had ever met. That was right before he disappeared on that expedition in South America when I was seven. He and my mom were there together, recording birdsongs, because he was a major bird fan too.

My mom was already out of the car, unloading the cage from the front seat.

"There are some reporters up there from the local TV station," the ranger explained to her. "Got cameras and everything. I guess this is a big story for all you bird nuts."

"We prefer to be called bird lovers," my mom said patiently.

I could tell she wanted to say more, but even if she had wanted to, no one would have heard her anyway over the sound of Lark screaming. Yup, when old Lark heard the word "reporter," she just couldn't contain herself. She let loose a shriek that nearly sent my eardrums into orbit.

"Reporters!" she screeched. "My fellow journalists!

Mom, you have to let me come with you. My whole career depends on it."

"I didn't know you could have a career in screeching," I said.

"Be nice, hotshot," Granny said, giving me a poke in the ribs. "She got carried away. It happens to us girls, doesn't it, Lark?"

"It happens to us *women*," Lark said, saying the word "women" as though she was the first person ever to say it. She must love the sound of that word, because it was like the twentieth time she had said it that day.

Here's a tip. If you ever meet my sister Lark, don't go calling any females *girls*, because she will come down on you like a sack of potatoes and crush you until you promise never to say the "g" word in her presence again.

On second thought, here's a better tip. If you ever meet my sister Lark, just head the other way. Oh, and run, don't walk.

You'll thank me, I promise.

CHAPTER 4

The Funkster's Funky Fact #4: In California, there is a law that says you cannot herd more than 3,000 sheep down Hollywood Boulevard at any one time.

It took some serious convincing, but Lark finally talked my mom into letting her go on the trek up to the Hollywood sign. There was one condition, though.

"I want you to leave your camera here," my mom said as she handed the cage to the ranger. "Heaven knows there are already enough cameras up there to frighten that bird out of his mind."

"But my camera is an essential tool for my blog," Lark protested, leaning over me and taking up what I considered to be way too much of my personal space. "It's like my right hand."

"No problem," I said with a chuckle, "because you're left-handed anyway."

"Daniel, did anyone ever tell you that everything is NOT a joke."

"I believe you've pointed that out, one or two million times."

Lark shot me one of her *boys-are-so-lame* looks,

but when she saw my mom leaving, she decided to ignore me.

"Fine, Mom," she reluctantly agreed. "I'll leave my camera here, but no one touches it and that means you, Daniel."

"Like I would want to anyway," I muttered. "It's covered with your eye slime."

Lark put her camera down on the seat and crawled out of the minivan. I reached out and knocked off one of her flip-flops just for the fun of watching her hop out of the car one-footed. It was pretty amusing. I think you would have enjoyed it too.

"If it's all right, maybe I'll join you two," Lola said. "Perhaps I can whisper some sacred Native American spirit words into his little eagle ears to soothe him, the poor dear."

"Last I looked, eagles don't have ears," my mom pointed out.

"Barbie wants to come too," Goldie said, jumping out of the car, clutching her doll to her chest. "She wants to show the eagle her new ponytail."

"I'm sure he'd love to see that, honey," my mom said.

Excuse me? Since when do bald eagles know anything about hairdos? After all, they're bald!

"Daniel, are you coming too?" my mom asked.

"We might as well make it a family excursion."

"I'll pass, Mom. I'm fine just watching you guys from the car."

She didn't push me to come, because she knows I'm not really into birds. In fact, they creep me out. All that wing-flapping and squawking and chirping and pecking gets me nervous. Plus, any animal that poops and flies at the same time gets a big *no thank you* in my book.

Granny and I climbed out of the way back and

leaned against the hood of the minivan, watching the four Funk women follow the ranger up the narrow dirt path that led to the sign. They were quite a sight. But you know what? Even I, The Funkster, had to hand it to them. Despite the fact that it was steep and dusty and rocky up there, not one of them made a peep. They just marched on up the hill, without one word of complaint. They're tough, those Funk females.

Weird, but tough.

We watched them for quite a few minutes. When they reached the sign at the top of the mountain, Granny Nanny decided to bail on me.

"Listen, hotshot, I'm going to meander over that a way for a few minutes," she said, pointing to a nearby ledge where a big leafy tree seemed to grow out of the rock. "That's where Muscles and I had our first kiss. He was a good smoocher, that one."

Suddenly, Pablo stuck his head out of my sweatshirt pocket.

"I heard that," he said. "The Pablo would prefer that there be no smoochy talk, if you please, Granny."

Granny looked surprised when she saw Pablo in my pocket.

"I thought I told you to stay home," she said to him.

"Oh," Pablo said. "I have to get my ears checked because I thought you said that I was *not* to stay home."

"Pablo Picasso Diego Funk!" she said, wagging her bony finger at him. "One day, you are going to have to learn to follow directions."

"Whoa there, Granny. I have explained to you that The Pablo is allergic to directions."

"You're impossible," Granny said to him. "Cute, but impossible. Now, can I trust you boys to stay put? I'm dying to see if my name is still on that tree trunk where Muscles carved it."

"We won't go anyplace," I assured her. "We love to stay put, don't we, Pabs?"

"Nothing I love more," Pablo said. "Not even mini-marshmallows with chocolate sauce. We'll see you in a few, Lou."

As Granny headed off to the nearby ledge, she seemed lost in a long-ago memory. For her sake, I hoped it was a good one.

Pablo grabbed on to the top of my sweatshirt pocket and pulled himself up with all his might. He craned his neck and took a look around. When he saw the Hollywood sign up on the hill, I thought his eyes were going to bug out of his head. Can you imagine what it looked like to him? I mean, those letters were huge to me and I was regular size. To someone only an inch tall, that sign must have looked totally, completely, incredibly humongous.

"Wow!" he said. "Check that out, scout!"

"It's pretty amazing, isn't it?"

"I can't believe it, bro. Here we are. Right smack in the middle of the real deal. Hollywood. The place where movie stars are made!"

"You got that right, Pabs."

"Wowie kazowie! I can just feel the glamour, can't you, dude? The opening night, the crowds of reporters trying to snap a picture, the red carpet. It's all right here on this hillside."

"I don't see any red carpet," I told him. "Just some green cactus."

"Dan, Dan, Dan." He slapped his forehead with the palm of his hand, a gesture I'd seen him do when he's really frustrated with something. "Where is your imagination, bro? Close your eyes. Feel the Hollywood vibe. Listen to the applause. Can you hear it?"

I closed my eyes and listened. I heard some bees buzzing. I heard a dog barking down in the canyon. And I'm pretty sure I heard my stomach growling, which was probably a reaction to the salami and green pepper sandwich I'd had for breakfast. But I didn't hear any applause.

Pablo could tell what I was thinking, which they say happens a lot with twins.

"I didn't mean actual applause, meathead," he said. "I mean the echo of Hollywood history, all those millions of fans, clapping for their favorite stars. Doesn't it make you want to be in the movies, Dan? To see yourself on the big screen?"

I laughed, but stopped suddenly when I noticed that Pablo wasn't laughing.

"Not me, Pabs. I could never be a star. I'm just a regular guy."

"Well, I could be a star if I wanted to be," he said, with a gleam in his eye that I hadn't seen before. "I have looks. I have personality. I even have a cape, dude. What more do you need?"

"A little thing called talent," I said. "Oh, yeah, and a camera. And that's just for starters."

"I have talent," he said. "Granny Nanny tells me that all the time."

By then, my mom and Lola and the sisters had reached the top of the mountain where the sign was. I could see my mom bending down and checking something out behind the Y. She was moving very slowly and cautiously, taking one step forward and then pausing for five or ten seconds. I knew she was trying to make contact with the eagle. All of her exams start with her making contact with the animal, because she says it's very important to establish a trusting relationship.

I can understand that with a dog or a cat, or even with a rabbit. I mean, you give a bunny a carrot or two and bamo-slamo, the little guy is a bundle of trust. But how you get a bald eagle to trust you is beyond me. Maybe you just have to tell him he looks really good without hair. That's what my mom always used to tell Uncle Morris, and it worked pretty well on him.

It was getting hot out there, and I was desperate to cool off. I suspected that building a trusting relationship with the eagle was not something that was going to happen super fast. So I took the opportunity to duck into the car for some shade. Since he was stuck in my pocket, Pablo had no choice but to come with me.

I flopped down on the middle seat and blew some air up toward my forehead to get a little breeze circulating under my hair. Just to be nice, I thought I'd blow a little air on Pablo too, to cool him off.

When I leaned down to find him, I saw that he had crawled out of my pocket. He was sitting very still on the seat of the car, just staring at something next to him. I glanced over to see what he was looking at.

It was Lark's camera. Lying there on the seat.

He looked at me and smiled. I swear to you, I truly believe I saw a little tiny lightbulb going off in Pablo's little tiny brain.

"The Pablo has an idea," he said.

Oh, no. I knew that sentence. I had heard him say it many times before. And the one thing I knew about that sentence was this:

It always came just before we got into trouble.

CHAPTER 5

The Funkster's Funky Fact #5: The zipper replaced buttons for fastening the fly in men's pants in 1937.

"Okay, Mister Dan, here's the plan," Pablo said before I even had time to be curious. "You're going to hold Lark's camera and The Pablo will stand up on the hood of the car. We'll make sure we can see the Hollywood sign very clearly in the background. Then you'll start filming and I'll perform."

"No deal," I said.

"Yes, deal," he shot back. "I'll just sing one song. And maybe do a little of that va-voom dancing Granny taught me."

"No way, Pabs." I said. "I am not recording you on this or any other camera. You're supposed to be a secret, remember? The last thing we need is to have you plastered all over the whole World Wide Web."

"Whoa there, bro. Easy does it. I have no intention of letting anyone see the video."

"Then why do it?"

"Let me remind you that we are here in front of the Hollywood sign," Pablo said. "How many times

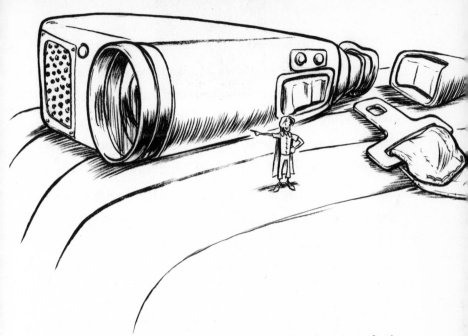

in our life is this going to happen? Besides, I'm feeling inspired."

"Well, uninspire yourself," I told him. "No deal."

"Listen, Dan my man. It's not dangerous. I have it all planned. We'll download the video to your computer the minute we get home."

He was really trying hard to convince me.

"We'll file it under some title that no one would ever want to see—like "Daniel Getting Potty Trained" or "Lark Gets the Stomach Flu." We'll be the only ones who know where it is. Trust me, bro. No one will ever see our little movie but you and me."

"And even we won't see it, because I'm not doing it."

"Fine," he sighed. "Go ahead and be the most boring brother this side of Wisconsin. See if I care."

I knew Pablo was steaming mad, and I understood why. What he was suggesting did sound like a lot of fun. You have to admit, having a movie of yourself performing in front of the actual Hollywood sign would be awesome. But as I was saying in the prologue (and friends, this is a pop quiz to see if you actually read it), I have a *life-and-death-secret* to keep (do those words sound familiar?). I couldn't mess around with that.

"No," I said to Pablo. "And that's final."

Pablo let out a huge groan, shook his head, and climbed back into my pocket. He refused to come out, even when I offered him a peppermint Tic Tac I found in my jeans pocket.

I popped the Tic Tac in my mouth and sat back to wait for Granny's return. Not thirty seconds had gone by when I felt something crawling on my sweatshirt sleeve. I looked down and saw Pablo climbing up my arm like he was scaling Mount Everest. When he reached my elbow, he took a flying leap and landed on my zipper, right smack dab on the metal pull tab. All our Curtain Crashers games had given him good aim.

"Well?" he said, putting his hands on his hips and staring up at my chin. "Are you going to pull me up or do I have to climb the whole way?"

I reached down and, being careful not to squish him, pulled the tab until my zipper was practically up to my neck. He climbed off and marched over to my shoulder. I could tell he meant business.

"This is how The Pablo sees it," he began. "You have one opinion and I have another. We need a fair solution, so I say we flip a coin."

"I don't have a coin."

"Wrong, bro. I happen to have spent the last half hour in your pocket. And I'm here to tell you that it contains one slightly used Kleenex, one already-been-licked Tic Tac, a broken pencil stub, a bubble gum wrapper with an extremely unfunny cartoon, and yes . . . one copper penny. Suitable for flipping."

I reached into my pocket and rummaged around for the penny. He was right. There it was, buried in the slightly used Kleenex.

"The answer is still no, Pabs."

"Think of me, your only brother," Pablo said, moving closer to my ear and talking in a low, sad voice. "Raised on my own, with no one but an elderly grandmother to play with, waiting for the moment when I could show my talent. You can make that happen, bro. With just a flip of the coin. What do you say? Do it for me."

I sighed. As I think I've mentioned before, it's

impossible to say no to Pablo, especially when he looks at you with those puppy-dog eyes.

"Okay," I said, pulling the coin out of my pocket. "Heads or tails?"

"Tails," he said, breaking out in a grin. "Flip it, dude."

I got out of the car. Pablo was hanging on to my shoulder and watched as I tossed the penny up in the air. It came down and landed right next to the front tire of our car.

I went over to look at it. As I bent down, Pablo flung himself off the zipper, doing a double somersault with a half twist before going into the full-on Pablo Plunge. Amazingly, he landed on a eucalyptus leaf right next to the penny.

TAILS!

"Tails," he hollered, pumping his tiny fist in the air.

Tails it was.

I shouldn't have given in. It was dangerous, making that video, and I knew it. But a deal is a deal, and there was no getting out of it now.

CHAPTER 6

The Funkster's Funky Fact #6: A men's regulation-sized basketball is 29.5 inches around and weighs 22 ounces.

I glanced up at the Funk women at the top of the mountain. Lola was squatting down next to the eagle, and my mom was edging the cage she had brought a little bit closer to him. She was wearing big gray gloves and looked like she was moving in slow motion. I could see the eagle flapping his wings as if to say, *Oh no you don't, lady. You're not going to handle me with those big gray gloves.* But my mom is pretty magical with birds, and I knew that somehow she'd be able to lure him into the cage so they could bring him down safely. That meant if we were going to make our video, we had to move fast before they came back.

Pablo was totally amped up. I plopped him on the hood of the car and went to the middle seat to get Lark's camera. When I returned with the video camera, he was looking at his reflection in the windshield, trying to tidy up. That wasn't going to be easy. Neither of us Funk boys is too strong in the grooming department.

"How's the look, bro?" he asked.

"It could use a little work."

Pabs shook the lint off his cape and tried running his fingers through his hair, which was its usual messy style. Granny doesn't make him comb it, so he has about ten years' worth of knots in it.

"I may give up on the hair," he said. "It's not cooperating."

"Good idea," I agreed. "Focus on fixing the face."

"What's wrong with my face, bro?"

"Nothing, if you like the wet look."

Pablo put his face up to the windshield and looked at himself closely.

"It's hot out here. So what if I got a little sweaty?" he said. "It makes me look kind of tough and manly, don't you think, bro?"

"Uh, more like grimy and gross."

"That's not good."

"Agreed. A little makeup might help," I suggested.

"Yo, brother of mine. You have been cooped up with females too long and they have taken over your brain. Dudes do not wear makeup."

"Dudes on TV do. You don't see the Jonas Brothers sweating like hogs."

Pablo thought about this for a minute.

"You got a point there, dude." He looked at himself in the windshield again, and this time, he didn't seem too pleased.

"Wait here," I said to him. "I have an idea."

I went back into the car and got Lola's purse from the front seat. Rummaging around in it, I located that silver compact she uses to powder her nose. She always told me it was given to her by a very wise man in China who said that the words inscribed on it say, "Pick a feather from every passing goose." I never quite got the wisdom of that saying, but that just shows you how little I know about geese, passing or otherwise.

I opened her compact and took out the fluffy powder puff on top, first rubbing it around in the compact to make sure it picked up a big blob of powder. Then I went back to the hood of the car where Pablo had made his hair look almost decent.

"Okay, superstar," I said. "Your makeup has arrived."

I reached out and patted Pablo with the powder puff. (Wow, try saying that ten times fast!)

It's a known fact that when you're only an inch tall, it doesn't take much to knock you over. A good swipe with a feather would probably do it. But I'm here to tell you, a thwack from a loaded powder puff will definitely send you reeling. As soon as that puff hit Pablo, he went over like a bowling pin, swallowed up in a tornado of beige dust. He rolled across the hood of the car, coughing and sputtering from inside his cloud of powder. Luckily, I caught him just as he was about to roll off the hood of the car.

"You got a heavy hand with the makeup!" he wheezed. He looked like he had fallen into a sack of flour.

By then, I was laughing so hard I almost dropped the camera.

"Pull yourself together," Pablo said. "I can't have my cameraman busting a gut."

"You just look so funny," I howled.

He burst out laughing too. I mean, why not? This was total fun.

I leaned down and blew on him. That worked really well, sending all the powder flying off him and into the air. Unfortunately, it also sent Pablo flying off into the air. He shot up like a helium balloon. It's a good thing I can jump, because a less athletic guy would not have been able to leap up and catch him in midair like I did.

"Woo hoo!" Pablo shouted. "That definitely rocked!"

I put him back down on the hood of the car and

he smoothed his hair for the second time that day. That was more hair-combing action than he'd had in his whole life!

"Let's do this," he said.

I focused the camera on Pablo, but stood far enough back so I could see the Hollywood sign in the background. I have to admit, it was a very cool-looking shot. There was Pablo standing in front of that majestic, huge, world-famous sign. It was definitely the kind of thing you don't see every day, or even every year, for that matter.

But what blew me away even more was his performance. Since I'd known Pablo for only a month,

I had no idea he could sing. But I'm here to tell you, that little guy could belt it out like a total rock star. Granny had taught him all her favorite songs from the old days, and he sang a song by this guy Elvis Presley, who was the first rock star ever.

Pablo was incredible. He shook his hips and shimmied his shoulders and played a mean air guitar as he sang. The song was "You Ain't Nothing but a Hound Dog," and it was about this weird dog that kept crying because he hadn't ever caught a rabbit. Don't ask me what those lyrics mean, because I couldn't tell you why anyone would want to sing about some dog catching a helpless little rabbit. But here's the deal: Pablo could have been singing in Pig Latin or Ancient Greek and he would still have been a knockout.

The kid had talent with a capital *T*. And style, too. Like when he came to the end of the song, he threw his arms up in the air, grabbed his cape with each hand, and dropped to one knee. Then he stood up and took a bow as if a million people were applauding him. At the end, he said, "Thank you very much. The Pablo is leaving the building," at which point he threw his head back, spun around on his teensy-weensy feet, and ran off the stage.

He was so good, he actually had me believing for

a minute that he was really on a stage and not on the hood of our minivan.

"Holy macaroni, Pabs," I said. "You're awesome!"

"Granny taught me to do that," he said. "She calls me her little Elvis."

"I can't even carry a tune," I said. "Looks like you hogged all the talent genes."

"Yeah, and you hogged all the height genes."

We laughed and high-fived each other, which I had to do very carefully so I wouldn't knock Pablo off the car and send him flying again.

"Let's do another song," he suggested.

I looked around and saw Granny coming down the trail and heading over to us. Then I looked up on the mountain and saw that my mom had the eagle in the cage, and was beginning to start down the path. Wow, I had missed all the bird action.

"There's no time now," I said. "You have to go back into your hiding spot."

"Can we just play back the video a little?" Pablo begged. "I'm dying to see it."

"Later," I promised. "We'll download it as soon as we get back from Robin's game. Now make like a tree and leave."

I held open the pocket of my sweatshirt so Pablo could jump in.

"No way, Jose," he said. "The Pablo is not going back into used-Kleenex land. That is no place for a star."

"Okay, okay. You can be in my shirt pocket. Just hurry up and get in."

I picked Pablo up and dropped him into my T-shirt pocket. I watched him gather up some blue lint into a little ball and settle down on it.

"The Pablo pillow," he called up. "I invented it."

By the time Granny returned, I had put Lark's camera back on the seat where I found it. I was just leaning against the car, chewing on a blade of grass, like nothing had happened. She looked really happy to see me. Or maybe she was just happy in general.

"It's still there," she said. "My name, carved in the tree trunk."

"That's so cool, Granny. It must feel great to see it after all those years."

"It does, hotshot. It's like looking at a little piece of my past."

I think she had a tear or two in her eyes as she reached out to give me a big hug.

"Ooowwwww," Pablo yelled from the pocket of my shirt. "Could you lighten up on the squeezing action, folks? The pressure is killing me."

Granny and I both laughed. "Your brother never was much of a hugger," she said.

It took only a couple of minutes for the rest of the Funk women to come down the path and arrive at the car. The ranger was carrying the cage with the eagle inside. That bird was flapping around like crazy, and I'm not embarrassed to tell you, the fierce look in his eyes made me extremely uncomfortable. Okay, downright scared. I hadn't realized how big those bald eagles can be. This one had a white head with a pointy orange beak, a body that was covered in blackish-brown feathers, and yellow legs with claws that were longer than Pablo even if he was standing on his tiptoes.

"Welcome to Hollywood, big fella," I said to him. He stared at me with those crazy eagle eyes.

"He doesn't like you, Daniel," Goldie said. "He just likes Barbie. They're best friends."

Two reporters were following my mom. One guy was right next to the cage, shooting a million pictures of the eagle. The other guy was bringing up the rear. I couldn't see him too well, but I heard him laugh when Goldie made her comment.

"She's adorable," he said to my mom.

Right. He should see her when she throws a tantrum because there aren't enough raisins in her

Raisin Bran. He'd change his mind real quick.

"Dr. Funk," the reporter with the camera said, when the party had reached our minivan. "Where are you taking the eagle?"

"I've called the Bird Rescue Center," my mom answered, "and they've agreed to put him in my care for observation. I'll be in phone consultation with the American Eagle Foundation until we figure out what's wrong with him."

"Contact me for details," Lark told the guy. "I'll be covering the minute-by-minute story on my blog."

Right, I thought. *We'll all be sure to check it out on I-Wouldn't-Know-An-Eagle-from-an-Elephant dot com.*

"Dr. Funk," the other reporter asked. "Do you plan to release the bird into the wild?"

Now that I could see him clearly, I realized that I knew that guy. I recognized him from the local news. He was the reporter who did all the really crazy goofy stories . . . like the ones where people dress their cat as Dracula for Halloween or set a world record for growing the world's largest cabbage in their backyard. His name was Harry Lipp, which I remembered because . . . well, let's face it . . . who wouldn't remember someone named Harry Lipp. Forgetting him would be like forgetting someone named Seymour Butts or Rusty Nail or I. P. Daily.

Anyway, Harry Lipp seemed really into the bald eagle story.

"I'm not sure yet what will happen to this bird, Mr. Lipp," my mom answered. "It depends. We certainly hope he's releasable, but that will depend on his condition. I'll be checking him for injuries to his eyes, his talons, and his wings. We have to determine if he's able to hunt and to fly."

"I'll have those minute-by-minute status updates on my blog," Lark told him, "complete with all the medical test results." Harry Lipp didn't pay much attention to her, which I thought was an excellent decision on his part.

"Barbie doesn't like to have medical tests," Goldie chimed in from nowhere. "She's afraid of shots."

Harry let out another one of those *isn't-she-cute* laughs and actually asked the cameraman to take a picture of Goldie kissing Barbie on her little plastic cheek. Give me a break. I mean, if they play *that* on the nightly news, I'll be the first one switching channels.

My mom asked the ranger if he could transport the eagle to our house. She explained that she couldn't take him herself because she had promised Robin we'd be at her game, and she never breaks a promise to us kids.

Harry Lipp watched the ranger load the cage into his truck. Good old Lark was on the poor guy like a barnacle on a whale.

"Did I mention I'm covering the volleyball championship for our school website?" she blabbed.

He didn't answer.

"I'm going to post a video of it on my blog. I hope you'll check it out."

"Sure thing," Harry said, which I think was code for . . . I'd rather hike across the North Pole barefoot in my Speedos.

"The name is Lark Sparrow Funk," she said, handing him one of her cheesy business cards. "Woman reporter."

I'm sure he didn't want it, but Harry Lipp seemed like a pretty decent dude, so he took the card and put it in his pocket.

As we got back into the minivan, my mom checked her watch.

"It's almost one," she said. "I hope there's no traffic."

We practically needed a crowbar to pry Lark away from Harry Lipp. Finally, she climbed into the car and the first thing she did was check out her camera. I tried to look the other way, but she squinted her eyes and gave me a suspicious stare.

"It's been moved," she said.

"Maybe it was trying to run away from you," I said with a shrug.

"Daniel, I asked you not to put your grimy little hands all over my camera. It is not a toy."

"I resent that, Larkster. My hands are not grimy or little. For your info, they are big enough to dribble a regulation basketball and I'll have you know, I washed them thoroughly yesterday morning. No, wait. I think it was the morning before, but still, that's only three days."

I heard Pablo laughing from deep inside my T-shirt pocket.

"You go, bro," I thought I heard him say.

I reached over and grabbed Lark's camera from her hands, just to make sure I got some of my finger dirt on it. It's fun to totally gross her out.

"Daniel, give that back!" she shrieked.

Just then, Harry Lipp stuck his face in the car to say good-bye.

"You like to do photography, son?" he asked, noticing that I was holding the camera in my hands.

"Sure," I said. "I'm really trying to improve my skills because I think photography is just about as interesting as anything I can think of, even more interesting than baseball or skateboarding or watching wrestling on TV."

I know what you're thinking. Daniel Funk, you don't give an owl's hoot about photography. But understand, folks. I was having a ton of fun watching Lark be horrified that I was handling her beloved camera. And the longer she was horrified, the more fun it was for me. Photography was as good a subject as anything to stretch out the time.

"Keep at it, son," Harry said. "It's a wonderful hobby, and maybe someday you'll make a career of it. What's your name?"

"Daniel," I said. "Nice to meet you, Mr. Lipp."

He was a really nice guy. You have to hand it

to someone who goes through life with a name like Harry Lipp. I wouldn't have wanted to be him on the first day of school, that's for sure.

"Let's hit the road," my mom said. "Good-bye, Mr. Lipp."

I think he said one last thing to me, but I couldn't hear him over the sound of the car engine revving up as we pulled away from the Hollywood sign and headed to the gym at John Burroughs High for Robin's volleyball game.

CHAPTER 7

The Funkster's Funky Fact #7: When volleyball was first invented in Massachusetts in 1895, it was called mintonette.

If you ask me, and I know you didn't, the less said about Robin's game, the better.

Let's face it, folks. In the wide world of competitive sports, eighth-grade girls' volleyball is not one of your more exciting events. Give me ultimate wrestling or extreme skateboarding or even a college football game, and I'm all over it. But sitting in a semi-stinky gym and watching a bunch of girls in pink shorts and ponytails hugging every time they make any kind of a decent shot is not my idea of athletics.

However, one interesting thing did happen at Robin's game.

Her team won.

They were the underdogs, and no one even thought they had a chance against the girl giants from Redondo Beach Prep. But to everyone's surprise, the Ocean Avenue Middle School team pulled off an upset victory, winning in straight sets.

"Please tell me that you recorded every second

of it," Robin said to Lark, as she came bouncing over to the bleachers after the victory. We had just watched her hug every player on her team at least forty-seven times, which, I swear, took longer than the match.

"This little camera got every single play," Lark said. "Complete with a running commentary from yours truly."

She wasn't kidding about that! Lark's commentary didn't run, it galloped! I mean, her mouth went non-stop during every nanosecond of Robin's tournament.

Call me crazy, but I believe that when viewing a

sporting event, you should keep your piehole shut and actually watch the game. But the Funk women do not agree. No, they believe you should talk all the way through the game and preferably about things that have nothing to do with it.

During Robin's volleyball match, for instance, Lark commented at length on each of the following items:

1. Her opinion that chewing on ice makes an irritating sound (I don't agree!)
2. Her views on why elbow skin is often itchy (I don't care!)
3. Her outlook on the future of short shorts in women's sports (I'm all for them!)

You'll notice that not one of these subjects has anything to do with volleyball, but did that stop her? Nope. At one point during the match, Pablo actually poked his head out of my pocket and said, "Dude, doesn't her mouth ever get tired?"

I kept Pablo's mind off the constant chatter by slipping a piece of popcorn into my pocket for him to munch on. That piece lasted him the whole tournament, which makes sense when you think about it. I mean, one piece of popcorn is almost half his size.

All the way home, everyone had to listen to Robin jabber her head off. It wasn't easy to take. I mean, how many times can you hear about Madison's *totally awesome* cross-court shot and Jillian's *totally awesome* spike and Spencer's *totally awesome* dig and Jennifer's *totally awesome* knee brace? (No kidding, friends. She actually said that.)

The only good thing was that Robin's chatter seemed to make the ride home go faster. I couldn't wait to get there and take a look at the video of Pablo. My mom had asked for one of us to help her take notes while she examined the eagle, and in a stroke of genius, I had volunteered Lark. I knew that would keep her busy for at least a half hour, which gave me plenty of time to borrow her camera and do the download. No one would ever know about the video. As Pablo would say, it was "easy peasy."

But here's a tip, friends. Strokes of genius don't always work out. I mean, how was I to know that one little giccup would change *easy peasy* into *double trouble*?

CHAPTER 8

The Funkster's Funky Fact #8: Ants can lift from 20 to 50 times their own body weight. If kids could lift as much as ants, they could hurl cars down the street.

The trouble began not long after we got home. I don't mean to blame Pablo, but it was partly his fault. Okay, it was *all* his fault. I mean, he was the one who said he was thirsty and wanted a Coke. Was it my fault if I took a sip?

Let me just tell you what happened, and you can be the judge.

When we got back to our house, everyone helped my mom carry the cage inside. The poor eagle looked plenty stressed and I can't blame him. The first thing he saw was our bulldog, Princess, leaping off the couch and bounding over to his cage to sniff him. Princess wouldn't hurt a flea (which is probably why she has so many of them), but the eagle didn't know that.

We put his cage up on the dining room table because my mom thought it was a good idea for him to hear our voices and get used to being among all of us. Robin went into the kitchen to sit in the breakfast nook and yak on the phone, which is how she spends ninety-nine percent of her time. Goldie went to give Barbie a manicure. Granny Nanny said she needed a nap, and Lola was off to her sweat lodge in the backyard. Lark went into her room to put her camera down and get a pencil and paper to take notes.

So much for Mr. Eagle being among all of us. It looked to me like he got stuck with my mom and yours truly.

I counted to two, then asked my mom to call Lark.

"You guys have to get this exam started," I said. "Every second counts when you're dealing with a nervous bird."

My mom smiled at me and tousled my hair.

"Why, Daniel, that's a very sensitive thing to say," she said. "I'm glad to see you're learning to love birds the way I do."

"I'm starting to feel very close to my feathered friends," I answered. I figured that was kind of true, because my best friend Vu Tran wears a necklace that Lola gave him with a Native American feather on it, which would technically make him my feathered friend . . . and I do feel very close to him.

When Lark came into the dining room, I was happy to see that she didn't have the video cam with her. The coast was clear. Except for one little detail. Lark didn't like me in her room, and sneaking in was going to be hard.

But fear not. The Funkster handled the situation brilliantly.

"While you guys check out the bird," I said, real casual-like, "I think I'll go in my room and do a little reading. Lark, could I borrow one of your books? Maybe one of your collections of women's poetry?"

I swear, Lark almost started to cry.

"Really, Daniel?"

"Sure. It's time I gave that stuff a try. I wouldn't mind getting in touch with my feminine side."

"Finally!" she said, throwing her arms around my neck and practically knocking me over. "I've been waiting for this moment, Daniel."

I let her hug me for a second, but then I broke away. First of all, I didn't want her to think that she could make this hugging business a regular habit. That was definitely not okay with me. And second of all, I didn't want her to crush Pablo, who was still in my T-shirt pocket.

"So, Lark," I said, unhinging her arms from my neck. "You and Mom just go ahead and take your time and I'll wander into your room and pick out a book."

"Pick whatever you'd like, Dan, but I highly recommend *Skipping Down the Womanly Path: My Soul Journey to Self-Knowledge.*"

"Sounds like a real page-turner," I said. I had to sprint out of there before I burst out laughing and blew my cover entirely.

As I headed toward the hall, Pablo popped out of my pocket.

"The Pablo is dying of thirst," he said. "That popcorn really parched me."

"I'm pretty thirsty myself," I said. "Let's swing by the fridge and see if there are any cold sodas."

"Oh, yeah. That's what I'm talking about," Pablo said.

We were in luck. Somebody had gone to the market and put two six-packs of soda on the refrigerator shelf. I pulled out a can of Coke. It looked so good that I wanted to open it right there, but Robin was still yakking up a storm on the phone, and hearing about the whole *totally awesome* game again was way too much for my ears. So I grabbed the Coke and took it into my bedroom.

I lifted Pablo out of my T-shirt and put him on top of my desk. He went to his little area and came back rolling Granny Nanny's old silver thimble, which he uses as a cup. Even though it's too big for him to pick up, he likes to fill it up and slurp the liquid like I do at the drinking fountain.

"Do your thing, chicken wing," Pablo said, motioning for me to pop the top off the can.

I yanked off the metal tab and poured a few drops of Coke into his thimble. He stuck his head in and gulped down several big mouthfuls.

"That's good stuff, bro," he said. "Have a swig."

I leaned back and took a long gulp from the can. Phew. It was bubbly. Immediately, I felt a huge giccup welling up in my throat.

Two things you should know about giccups. First, they are an equal combination of a gargle, a burp, and a hiccup. And second, they make me shrink. Who knows why . . . it just is what it is.

Well, that, my friends, is exactly what happened. Before I could stop myself, that big, loud, watery giccup came flying out of my throat like a rocket ship. And that giccup set off a chain reaction that I had become very familiar with.

My eyeballs started to growl.

My fingers buzzed.

My nose bubbled.

And my knees let out a giant whistle.

Bamo-slamo! Down I went. Before I could even say "Excuse me" I had shrunk down to the size of a toe, and was standing on my desk, eyeball to eyeball with Pablo.

"What's buzzin', cousin," he said, bumping his tiny fist up against mine. "You up for a round of Curtain Crashers?"

"I can't, Pabs. We have to go get Lark's camera."

"What's the rush?"

"The rush is that we need to get your part of the video off of there before she posts the game stuff on her blog," I said. "I have only a half hour to do it, so I can't hang out and play now."

"The Pablo is disappointed," he said. "But a man has to do what a man has to do. Go to it, bro."

I opened my desk drawer. The Santa Claus pepper shaker was there, but it was too heavy for me to pick up, so I got out the feather that I keep there for times when I need to make myself sneeze. I handed it to Pablo, and he wiggled the feather under my nose. It tickled, and I sat back and waited for the sneeze that would unshrink me.

Nothing happened.

"What gives, bro?" Pablo asked. "Where's the sneeze?"

"I don't know. Tickle me again."

Pablo wiggled the feather under my nose. Still nothing. Not even the tiniest itch, nose-wise.

"Let me try," I said, taking the feather from him and desperately rubbing it all over my face. I don't know what had happened, but I can tell you this. There was no action in the sneeze department.

"We have to find Granny," I said. "She'll help us with the pepper shaker."

"She's taking a nap in her room, remember?"

Granny's room is in what used to be a sun porch in back of the kitchen. Sometimes we borrow Ken's four-by-four from Goldie's Barbie Dream house and drive there, because it's at least an hour walk when you're the size of a toe. But good old Robin was still blabbing away in the kitchen. If she saw Ken's jeep cruising across the linoleum, she'd rat us out for sure.

Pablo and I must have tried at least a hundred more times to make me sneeze. Nothing was working.

I tickled my nose with the curtain fringe. That was just annoying. I crawled under my bed to look for dust balls. No luck. Lola had vacuumed there the day before and had turned it into a dust ball–free zone. I got so desperate, I even stuck my nose in Stinky Sock Mountain. The smell made my eyes water but not a thing happened to my nose.

I thought about taking the four-by-four down to Lark's room and just dragging the camera away. But then I realized there was no way I could lift it.

"I wish I was an ant," I told Pablo, "so I could carry that video camera down here on my back."

"Well, I'm glad you're not an ant," Pablo said, "because I happen to know that ants only live forty-five to sixty days and if you died, I would miss you like crazy."

Wow. Pablo could say the nicest things when you least expected it.

My sneeze switch was in the off position and there was not a thing I could do about it.

Almost two hours went by. I was totally exhausted. It's a known fact that trying to sneeze for two hours takes a lot out of a guy. Don't try it at home, kids.

"Look," Pablo said, pointing to the door of my room.

I noticed that it was open a crack and our cat Sam was slinking in. (By the way, in case you were thinking that Sam is a boy, forget it. Sam's real name is Samantha, and like every other creature in our house, she's female.) Sam likes to come to my room just to creep out Cutie Pie, my Siamese fighting fish. It's one of her hobbies, along with licking her paws for hours on end and meowing for no reason at all.

Anyway, I watched her sneak over to Cutie Pie's bowl and stare into it, twitching her whiskers the way cats do.

Suddenly it hit me. Whiskers! That was the answer.

"Here, Sam," I called.

Cats have incredible hearing, so even though my voice was tiny, Sam came leaping over to me. She jumped up to the desk and meowed. From where I was sitting, she looked like a tiger. I had never realized what long teeth she had.

"Come closer," I said to her. She put her head down right next to me and twitched her whiskers, just like she had with Cutie Pie. I stuck my face up and let her whiskers pass back and forth across my nose. I started to feel something, an itch in the upper nose area. And then suddenly . . .

"Ah chooooooooooooo!"

I sneezed so hard I thought my nose was going to blast off to the moon.

And just like that, I shot up to my full size.

"Go to it, bro," Pablo said.

Without wasting a second, I jumped off my desk and went racing to the dining room table. My mom was holding the eagle with one of her gloved hands, and with the other hand, was trying to listen to the eagle's chest with a stethoscope.

"Ssshhhh," she said when she saw me. "Don't frighten him. It's taken me two hours to try to calm him down."

"Where's Lark?" I whispered.

"In her room," she whispered back. "I think our bird is doing much better. No broken wing, no visible wounds. I have to check him for parasites."

"That's great, Mom."

I raced out of the room and down the hall to Lark's room. I knocked frantically on her door and stuck my head in at the same time.

"Daniel," she said. "I was looking for you. You forgot to take this." She held out the *Womanly Skipping* book to me, or whatever it was called.

"Thanks, Lark. I can't wait to get started." I was trying to sound all casual but my heart was beating fast. "By the way, you don't happen to have your video camera around, do you?"

"Of course, it's right here. I've just finished downloading all the video of Robin's game onto my blog."

I gulped.

"So, like . . . did you . . . um . . . watch it all?"

"Don't be a moron, Daniel. That would take forever. It just takes a couple of clicks and it's done. We modern women know our way around a computer, you know."

"So let me get this straight, Lark. You posted everything that was on there? As in everything?"

"Why wouldn't I?" she asked. "Why? Is there a problem?"

A problem? Now there was a video of Pablo, my top secret mini-brother, splashed all over the entire Web for the whole world to see.

Yeah, I'd say that was a problem.

CHAPTER 9

The Funkster's Funky Fact #9: The longest one syllable word in the English language is "screeched."

I was in a total twist by the time I got back to my room, and my mind was racing a mile a minute, trying to think of a way out of this. Pablo was inside my LEGO castle, where he likes to hang out in the turret and pretend he's a guard.

"Who goes there?" he said when I tapped on the turret with my finger.

"We're in trouble, Pablo. Knock off the castle talk."

He stuck his head out the window, and I noticed that he was wearing a breast plate and holding a shield that he had swiped from one of my LEGO guys.

"Do you bring word from the king?" he asked. "How goes my lord?"

"Give it up, Pabs," I said. "This is serious."

"Methinks I understand," he said. "I shall open the drawbridge and make you welcome."

He climbed down the circular stairs of the turret

and arrived at the castle gate. Turning the little crank, he lowered the drawbridge and walked out. I noticed he had taken off his costume and put down his shield.

"What's up, pup?" he said.

"We're too late," I told him. "Lark posted your video on her website."

"You sure, bro?"

"That's what she said."

We went on my computer to check things out. Sure enough, when we went to Lark's website, there it was—the video of Pablo singing in front of the Hollywood sign, followed by the coverage of Robin's volleyball match.

"Man, do I look cool or what?" Pablo said. "Let's show Granny. She'll be so proud."

"Are you kidding? She'll be furious. No one is supposed to know about you, Pabs. Now everyone can see you."

"Who's everyone?" he said. "Come on, dude. We both know that no one looks at Lark's blog except Lark. And if there happens to be one or two Lark fans who see it, you can just tell them it was you, horsing around. We're identical, remember?"

"Right. And how do I explain the fact that I'm one inch tall?"

"You're smart, bro. You'll figure something out."

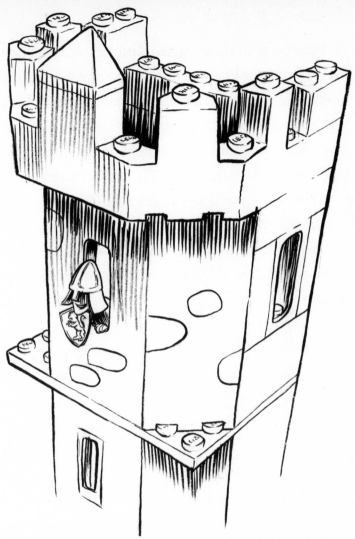

Pablo scooted across the drawbridge and disappeared back into the LEGO castle. I sat down in my blue leather La-Z-Boy recliner to think things through. It's where I get my best thinking done. I popped my feet up to the recline position and tried to clear my head.

Pablo did have a point. Basically no one even knew about Lark's blog. Any serious volleyball fan would go on the coach's site and check out the real highlights, the ones that don't have Lark's mouth running all the way through. And about her friends, the two other girls in the Women's Poetry Society were so geeky that I could just tell them how much I love skipping down the womanly path to self-knowledge, and they'd buy anything I told them after that.

Little by little, these thoughts calmed me down. I came to the conclusion that I had made this website thing a bigger deal than it really was.

"Pablo," I called out. "I'm better now."

He stuck his head out the window of the turret.

"Doth my lord care to come into the great hall and have a mutton chop and a glass of grog?" he said.

What'd I tell you about him? All play, all the time.

"I would be honored," I said, bowing to him. "Let me just tend to the horses, sire."

I was in the middle of pretending to tie up my imaginary horses, when I heard Lark scream. I think we all know that the girl has some serious lung power, but this scream was a real eardrum-splitter. I'd call it a screech.

"This is incredible!" she screeched. "You guys won't believe this!"

I stuck my head out of my room and saw my mom charging into the hall from the dining room.

"Lark, honey, no screeching. You're scaring the eagle. He needs to hear a soothing tone of voice."

"But Mom," Lark screeched again. "I have some amazing news!"

By then, Granny Nanny was up from her nap and Lola had come in from her sweat lodge. Even old Robin had gotten off the phone, which is a total miracle in itself.

"What's all the screeching about?" Granny Nanny asked.

"Harry Lipp just called me," Lark said.

"Eeuuww," Robin groaned. "Lip hair is so gross."

"He's a reporter, Robs," Lark explained.

"Whatever. He still should have laser hair removal."

Sometimes I love that Robin. It's fun to see how much she can frustrate Lark.

"Will everyone just listen for a minute?" Lark said, pretty frustrated already. "He called to say that he went to my site and watched the video I shot today. He loved it. And he's going to do a story on it tonight on the six o'clock news."

"You mean on television?" I said. I could hear my voice cracking as I spoke.

"Yup," Lark answered. "With millions of people watching."

"Mom, was I sweating during the game?" Robin asked, sounding suddenly panicked. "Because if anyone sees me on TV and I'm sweating in the armpit area, I'll just die."

"Did he say what part of the video he loved?" I asked Lark quietly.

"I'm sure he loved it all," Lark said. "But now that I think of it, he did mention something about a part near the beginning being really exceptional."

There they were. The dreaded words. *A part near the beginning.*

"How long before the news is on?" I asked. I was feeling sick to my stomach.

"Half an hour," Lola said. "Let's order some hummus and pita bread and Greek olives and all watch it together."

"Great idea, Lola," Robin said. "Except for the hummus part. That stuff is so beige and gross and everything. I vote for pizza instead."

"But no anchovies," Goldie chimed in. "Barbie hates anchovies."

"This is going to be wonderful," my mom said. "Isn't it exciting, Daniel?"

I didn't answer. Three words just kept rolling around in my head.

Millions of people. Not two people. Not hundreds of people. Not even thousands of people. But *millions* of people. Who were going to have *millions* of questions about my mini-brother.

The show was a half an hour away. There was nothing I could do to stop it. Once it was on, the secret of Pablo's existence would be out. Millions of people would know about him.

I was toast.

CHAPTER 10

The Funkster's Funky Fact #10: The very first Barbie doll was introduced at the American International Toy Fair in New York in 1959. That makes Barbie more than fifty years old!

When I told him what had happened, Pablo refused to be upset.

"I'm going to be a star, bro," he said. "Just like I dreamed of."

He's a very positive guy, and he just wouldn't believe that going public was going to be the end of his freedom. But I knew Granny was right. When people became aware that there was a kid in this world the size of a toe, Pablo would never be left alone again. I didn't know what would happen to him, but way down deep, I knew it was nothing good.

And what about my mom? How was she going to feel, learning that she had a secret mini-son? And what a way to learn a thing like that . . . from the six o'clock news! Suddenly, I wished I had told her everything from the very beginning, when I first started to shrink and discovered Pablo.

But the news was starting at six, and I couldn't turn back the clock. The pizza had been ordered, chairs had been gathered around the TV, and the Funk women were buzzing.

"I want to be there to see it," Pablo demanded. "It's my debut. Hey, by the way, you don't happen to have a red carpet I can walk down, do you?"

"This isn't going to be pretty," I told him. "Granny will be furious, Mom will be shocked, Lark and Robin will have a screech fest, and you'll probably scare the stuffing out of Goldie."

"Bro, look on the bright side for a change."

I tried to look on the bright side, but I just couldn't see it. All I saw was trouble ahead.

"Promise me one thing," I asked him. "Let me do the talking. Don't show your face until I tell you to. The shock will be too much for everyone."

I was remembering the first time I shrunk and saw Pablo. I took one look at him and fainted right there on the spot.

I put Pablo in my T-shirt pocket and headed out to the living room. Everyone was there, and the six o'clock news was just beginning. I sat down in the one remaining chair and thought how my life was never going to be the same again.

The anchorman went through the usual headline stories, which I couldn't hear because it was the same time that the pizza was being delivered at the

front door and Lark was complaining that they put sausage on it and she doesn't eat sausage. About halfway through the program, Harry Lipp came on to do his story.

"Ssshhh, everyone. Here it is," Lark said. "My first moment of fame as a reporter."

I put my head in my hands. I couldn't watch. I could feel Pablo jumping around in my pocket. I knew he was scaling up to the top so he could see out.

"This is a story about a remarkable family I met today, the Funks of Venice, California," Harry began. "At the head of this talented clan, there's Marci Funk, a local veterinarian who found herself at the Hollywood sign, rescuing a trapped bald eagle."

I peeked out from between my fingers to catch a glance at the TV. There was Mom in her big gray gloves, trying to coax the nervous eagle into the cage. I allowed myself to breathe just a little bit. Maybe this story wasn't going to be about Pablo at all.

"Then we have Robin Funk," he went on, "unlikely star of the Ocean Avenue Middle School volleyball team who today led her squad of eighth graders to the championship of the league."

There was a shot of Robin, jumping at the net and slamming a great spike to the opposing team.

"Please tell me you can't see any sweat," she said, barely able to look at the screen.

"Perspiration is a very natural thing, Robbie," Lola said. "In Finland, people sit nude in saunas just to make themselves sweat. It's very liberating."

"And very disgusting," Goldie added.

I was starting to relax. Harry Lipp didn't seem to be talking about Pablo at all. He was covering the eagle story and the volleyball tournament. What a relief.

"But the most remarkable member of the Funk family is young Daniel Funk. Take a look." Was he talking about *me*? What did I do?

The TV screen filled with the video of Pablo on the hood of the car.

"Look, Barbie! There's Daniel in a Batman cape," Goldie screamed.

I told you Pablo and I were identical. We were even fooling Goldie.

"This talented young man is a photographer and special effects wizard," Harry went on. "And as you can see, a pretty terrific little singer, too."

Did he say I was a special effects wizard? I love to watch all those behind the scenes DVDs about how they do special effects in movies, but I wouldn't have a clue how to do them.

Wait a minute. Wait . . . a . . . minute.

Suddenly, it hit me. Holy macaroni! Harry Lipp thought Pablo was a special effect! That would explain why he was only one inch tall, like the shrinking kids in that movie I can't remember the name of.

If you ask me, and I know you didn't, this was an incredible stroke of luck for Pablo and me. Harry Lipp had provided a perfect explanation for the video.

They showed Pablo's entire song on TV, every-thing we shot. There he was, standing on the hood of the car singing his amazing version of "Hound Dog," shaking his pea-sized rump like a spoonful of Jell-O—with the beautiful Hollywood sign in the background. I wish you could have seen it, friends. As Robin would say, it was *totally awesome*.

I shot a nervous glance at Granny, who was definitely not happy. She met my eyes with a look that said *how could you have let this video happen, Daniel? Now our secret is out!*

"Don't ask me how young Daniel Funk made this incredible video," Harry continued. "But he told me he loves photography, and this clip shows that he has some pretty good digital tricks up his sleeve. That little guy standing on the car looks as real as the nose on my face."

"And a whole lot better, too," I heard Pablo say.

"I didn't know you could do special effects, honey," my mom said.

"That's only one of the things you don't know about me, Mom."

"What I don't get," Lark said, "is how you were in front of the camera and behind it at the same time. You'd have to be two people."

Wouldn't you know that The Larkster would be the one to ask the hard questions? But I thought fast.

"Like the man says, Larkie, I have some pretty good tricks up my sleeve."

"Nice fake, bro," I heard Pablo say.

"So what we're seeing here is a talented family at work," Harry Lipp said, smiling into the camera. "And in conclusion, let me just say, an adorable one too."

Then they flashed a shot of Goldie, kissing Barbie on the cheek.

"Look, Barbie. We're famous!" Goldie shouted. I didn't have the heart to point out to her that Barbie was already pretty famous on her own.

"What about ME!" Lark said. "He didn't show me!"

"Sure he did, sweetheart," Lola said. "You were

right there in the background, when Goldie was kissing Barbie."

"Don't worry about it, honey," my mom said. "Good reporters are supposed to be behind the scenes."

"That is not fair," Lark said. "First the sausage, now this." She flicked off the TV and stormed off into her room.

Lark was not a happy camper. But me, I was the happiest kid in the universe. Pablo and I had stood on the very edge of big-time trouble, and we had come back from the edge. Saved by the magic of special effects.

CHAPTER 11

The Funkster's Funky Fact #11: Male Siamese fighting fish must be kept in separate tanks or they will fight each other, often to the death.

I wasn't prepared for what happened next. The phone started ringing and didn't stop until midnight.

Everyone I had ever met, and plenty of people I hadn't, called to say how great I was, that my performance on TV was killer, that I truly was a special effects wizard and one of the most talented performers they had ever seen. I swear, I must have gotten a million calls.

Well, maybe not a million, but at least ten, and that's a lot of phone time. By the end of the night, my right ear was beet red from having the phone squished against it for so long.

Some of the calls were awesome, like when my cousin Cole called from his college dorm and had his whole baseball team shout, "Congratulations, Dan, you're the man!" Others were a little strange, like when my best friend Vu Tran called.

"Hey, Dan, so how come I never knew you could sing?" he asked.

"When you have talent like mine, Vu, you hate to show off."

"But didn't Ms. Peacock in preschool ask you to just mouth the words to 'The Wheels on the Bus' so you wouldn't throw the rest of us off-key too?"

"That's absolutely correct, Vu, which just shows you what a poor choice of song 'The Wheels on the Bus' was for my particular voice. Especially the 'beep beep beep' part. It wasn't for me."

I thought Pablo would be really glad to know what a smash hit we were, so after each call, I'd go into my room and give him a full report. But as I told him about each call, I noticed he was getting grumpier and grumpier.

"You're not going to believe this one," I said to him, coming back into our room after one of the calls. Pablo didn't even look up this time. He was practicing his tightrope walking on a thread Granny had strung across my desk from my stapler to my scotch tape dispenser. He balances himself by holding a toothpick in front of him and tries to walk all the way across without falling.

"Not now, bro. Concentrating."

I couldn't wait until he was finished. I was too pumped up.

"That was Principal Quirk on the phone," I

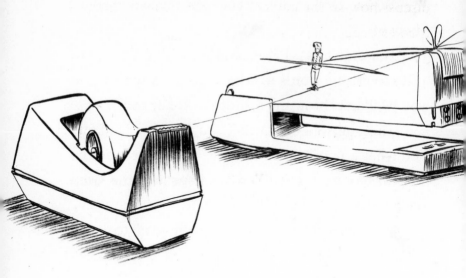

blurted. "He saw the video on the news and asked if I would speak at the school assembly this week."

Plop! Pablo fell off the thread and landed on the pink eraser down below. He got up, rubbing his butt where he had landed.

"And what exactly do *you* have to speak about?" he asked. He sounded mad, but I thought it was just from having fallen.

"He wants my topic to be 'The Special Kid Behind the Special Effects.' He thinks I should talk about how all the parts of my personality contributed to me learning to do what I do."

"Just one minor point," Pablo said. "You don't know beans about special effects. So maybe you can discuss how all the parts of your personality contributed to being able to fake it."

Ouch. That didn't feel good.

"Hey, Pabs. That wasn't cool."

"Well, how do you expect me to feel, bro? I'm the one who was a hit on TV, and you're the one getting all the attention."

"We're a team, Pabs. It's *us* getting the attention, not just me."

"Oh, really? Because I haven't noticed anyone calling *me* to ask *me* to speak at any assemblies."

"That's because they don't know you exist."

"My point exactly," he said. "I rest my case."

Wow, this was sounding like a real argument. I hated fighting with Pablo.

"Daniel, telephone again!" my mom called, sticking her head into my room. "By the way, did I hear you talking to someone?"

"Just starting to practice my speech for the assembly, Mom. Who's on the phone?"

"It's someone named Lanny Lambert," she said. "He says he's a friend of Harry Lipp's, and he wants to make you an offer you can't refuse, whatever that means."

"Okay, Mom. Could you tell him I'll be right there, please?"

She nodded and closed the door.

"Let me just take this call," I said to Pablo. "Then we'll get to the bottom of this."

The door opened again and my mom stuck her head in.

"Get to the bottom of what?" she asked, using her Supermom ears to pick up what I was saying.

"Um . . . um . . ." I looked around my room, and then luckily, my eyes landed on our Siamese fighting fish, Cutie Pie.

"I was just telling Cutie Pie that she should get to the bottom of her bowl because there's a few leftover fish flakes there that I think she should eat because she's looking a little on the bony side to me. But hey, I guess all fish are bony."

Shut up, Dan, I told myself. *Quit while you're ahead.*

Quickly, I followed my mom to the kitchen and picked up the phone.

"Daniel Funk here," I said. "Boy superstar."

I know, that was obnoxious. But listen, dudes, you have to have a little fun with fame, or what good is it?

"Lanny Lambert here," said the voice on the other end of the phone. "Producer, director, writer, and all around showbiz whiz."

Whoa, that was cool. I had never talked to a showbiz whiz before.

"I saw you on TV, Dan," he said, talking a mile a minute, "on that feature story my pal Harry Lipp did. Matter of fact, Harry called me up and told me to watch. Said he thinks he discovered a brand-new talent I might want to work with."

"Oh," I said. "Who's that?"

"You, baby. You can sing, you can dance, and I love the miniature special effects thing. It's a winner concept. People love little things, like ants, for example, or Matchbox cars or babies."

This guy was a real motormouth. I think if there were a world championship of talking, he might even beat out Lark, and that's saying something.

"So if it's okay with your family, I'd like to drop by tomorrow," he continued without any pause, "say around eleven, and pay you a visit. Talk showbiz. I think I can make you an offer that will blow your socks off."

"What kind of—"

"I'm a person with vision, and I'm seeing us start out with a guest spot on television," he said, before I had even finished the question. "Maybe one of those talent shows where people get discovered. You'll have to appear on video of course, because of the miniature thing, but hey, you're going leave the technical stuff to me, your writer-producer-director."

"That sounds—"

"Then I think we hit 'em with an MTV video," he interrupted, "which will lead to a recording contract. I feel confident that within a year, I'll be directing you in your own movie. I can see the headline now: 'Little guy hits big screen.' How's that sound, Dan?"

"Gee, Mr. Lambert . . . I'm not sure I have that kind of talent."

"Talent, schmalent. You got what it takes, baby. You're cute. People love you. And that's the key ingredient to becoming a star."

"Well, it sure would be fun to be a star."

"Perfect," he said. "I'll come by for brunch tomorrow. I'll bring the bagels, you bring the cuteness."

Click. He was gone.

When I told my mom about the call, she said she wasn't at all sure she was going to allow me to meet with Lanny Lambert. She said she had no idea who he was, and if he was even for real. I suggested she call Mr. Lipp at the television station and check him out.

"He's one of my best friends," Mr. Lipp assured her, after we had gotten him on the phone. "Lanny Lambert is a very talented producer, I'll tell you that. That guy has made some of this station's biggest hits, like *America's Funniest Pets* and *Dance Your Feet Off*."

"That's extremely impressive," my mom said.

"The guy talks a blue streak," Mr. Lipp went on, "but he gets things done. If anyone can help your kid become a star, he can."

After the phone call, my mom and I checked Lanny out on Google, and sure enough, he had a long list of shows he'd produced. It looked like he really was a showbiz whiz.

"How about it, Mom? Can I meet with him?"

She didn't answer. She was busy putting some vitamin drops into the eagle's water dish. When she still didn't respond, I actually volunteered to help her change the newspaper at the bottom of the eagle's cage. I thought that might soften her up. I mean, it was a real sacrifice for me. As much as I'm not a bird fan, I'm even less a fan of their droppings.

"Daniel," my mom said, when we were done cleaning the cage. "If I let you meet with Lanny, I want you to assure me that you're just going to listen to what he's suggesting. No decisions, just listen."

"I'll be all ears, Mom."

"And a second thing. He can only stay until noon, because we're busy after that."

"Busy with what?" I asked. "What could be more important than my future career?"

"Mr. Eagle here," she said, giving the bird a big smile. He just stared at her with those yellow eyes of his. I guess they were kind of beautiful—if you're into yellow eyes, that is.

"The good news is I have found nothing wrong with

LIN OLIVER

the eagle," she went on. "No broken bones showed up on the x-ray, no diseases, no injuries. We believe that the bird may have mistaken the Hollywood sign for a cluster of trees. And when he tried to land, he got stuck in the cables that hold the Y up."

I shot a glance over at the eagle. Now he was staring at me. If you ask me, and I know you didn't, it wasn't a totally friendly stare, either.

"You should learn to read, buddy," I said to him. "Then you'd know there's no Y in 'tree'."

"So after speaking with the American Eagle Foundation," my mom went on, "we've decided that he is healthy enough to be released back into the wild."

"And you've got to do that at noon? What's wrong with later?"

The eagle turned his gaze to me, and I swear, he was giving me some major attitude.

"Daniel," my mom said. "I hope I've raised you to understand that caring for our bird friends takes priority over everything."

I told you she was a certifiable bird nut. I'm talking showbiz and she's talking feathers.

"You know what I always say, Mom. Birds first."

"Good," she said with a smile. "Now just as a precaution, I'm going to attach a little tracking device to his leg, to make sure he doesn't lose his way again. I've arranged for the representatives from the Bird Rescue Center to be here at noon to observe, which is why Mr. Lambert will have to be gone by then."

I knew I couldn't argue with my mom when it came to the subject of birds, especially this eagle who seemed to have worked his way into her feather-loving heart. So I just decided then and there that an hour with Lanny Lambert was going to be enough time for him to make me an offer I couldn't refuse.

I ran back into my room to tell Pablo about the phone call with Lanny. He just listened quietly.

"It's what you wanted, Pabs," I said to him when he didn't answer. "A music video. A movie. The red carpet. The whole deal. You'll be a star."

"You'll be a star," he said. *"I'll* be unknown."

"You can't think of it that way, Pabs."

"Then maybe you can tell me how I should think of it, bro."

I didn't have an answer for that. He was right, and I knew it.

CHAPTER 12

The Funkster's Funky Fact #12: The longest limousine in the world is 100 feet long, has 26 tires, a heated Jacuzzi, a sundeck, a swimming pool, and a helipad!

Lanny Lambert arrived at our house the next day in a humongous black limousine. It was as long as our whole block. Okay, maybe not that long, but at least as long as our living room.

Vu was hanging out at our house. He claimed he came over to borrow my social studies book, but I think he just wanted to get a look at Lanny. I can't blame him. It's not every day a big-time producer drops in for bagels.

Lanny got out of the car and came up the front steps. He was wearing a baseball cap and a leather bomber jacket and had a silver-and-turquoise ring on every finger of his right hand.

"There he is," he said, pointing at me. "Ready for your close-up, Mr. Funk?"

He put out his right hand to bump fists, and when we did, I actually screamed, "Ouch!" Here's a tip: Next time a big Hollywood producer wants to bump fists with you, make sure he isn't wearing a lot of sharp rocky metal rings on his fingers. And if he is, here's another tip. Wear gloves.

"Are you Dan's sidekick?" he said to Vu.

"Yeah, I'm his best friend, Vu Tran."

"Well, Vu, your buddy here is about to take the ride of his life," Lanny said.

"In that limo?" Vu asked. "Cool. Can I come?"

Lanny laughed. "Actually, I wasn't referring to the limo, Vu. I was referring to Dan's showbiz career. But hey, if you guys want to take a limo ride, let's give it a whirl. What do you say? Might as well get used to the good life, huh, Dan?"

My mom was busy with her Bird Center pals. They were gathered around the cage, putting the tracker on the eagle's leg. When I asked her if we could go on the limo ride, she said Lola would have to go with us so she could continue her work.

Naturally, all three of the Funk sisters horned in on the action too. I don't suppose you care, because I know I didn't, but Robin insisted on putting on a cute new lavender outfit for the occasion. Lark announced that she wasn't taking her video camera, because she had given up the reporter's life. It was just too disappointing. You can read her farewell blog on thank-heavens-she's-finally-closing-her-piehole dot com. Goldie brought Barbie along, all dressed in her Hollywood Look with rhinestone sunglasses and strapless gown. Obviously, my talk with Goldie about monster trucks hadn't worked.

We all piled in to the huge horseshoe-shaped backseat of the car—everyone except Barbie, who rode in the front seat with the driver. Poor guy. He didn't look happy about that.

We cruised around the neighborhood for about ten minutes. Lola talked to Lanny about her favorite television show, *World Culture Digest*. (Oh, don't even ask how boring it is, because there isn't a word in the English language that could cover it except maybe *totally-boring-to-the-max-times-a thousand-million-billion*, and we all know that's not a word).

We played with every single thing in the car. We opened and closed the tinted windows, opened and closed the sunroof, took handfuls of the lemon drop candies that were overflowing from a bowl on the wooden panel next to our seats. I gulped down one of the free bottles of icy cold water and Robin helped herself to a can of Diet Coke that was in the little fridge. We even blew our noses in the free Kleenex, which smelled like strawberry-lime gum. It was cool.

If you're any kind of a decent person at all, you're probably wondering why I didn't ask Pablo to come along. Don't blame me. I wanted to but I couldn't find him.

I looked in all his hangouts . . . in the LEGO castle, in the Barbie Dream House Jacuzzi, in the geode on my desk where he likes to rock climb. I even asked Granny Nanny where he was. She told me last time she saw him, he said he had a lot to think about and was going to sit in the little teepee house she made him out of twigs and an old pair of my moccasins. When I looked, he wasn't there.

After we got back from the neighborhood cruise, Lanny Lambert came inside. We sat down at the breakfast nook in our kitchen and he took some bagels and cream cheese out of a brown bag. I got some plates and we had a little brunch. The nook was a busy spot because my mom and the bird people were going back and forth, taking the eagle cage outside to the backyard to get ready for the great bird launch.

Lanny didn't seem to mind the action, though. He just gulped down his bagel and cream cheese and talked. It's not easy to chew a bagel and talk nonstop but, trust me, the guy had that combo down pat.

"So, Dan," he said. "You can tell me. How'd you do it, make yourself look little?"

"Would you like some more cream cheese, Lanny?"

He shook his head. "Obviously the little guy is you," he continued. "But did you use animation or digital effects or what?"

For a second, I thought about telling him the truth. That I happen to have an identical mini-brother who is an Elvis impersonator. But I decided not to. I didn't want him gagging on his bagel.

"Who taught you how to do the Elvis thing?" he went on without even waiting for an answer. "I'm all ears."

Here was a question I could answer. I explained to him about Granny Nanny and how she loved Elvis Presley. By the time I finished, he was done with his bagel. He moved in close to me, and lowered his voice to a whisper.

"I'll be up-front with you, Dan. I want to make a deal with you. I've seen stars come and go, but I think you have lasting power. What do you say? Do you want to be partners?"

Boy, did I ever!

He put his hand out. As I reached over to shake it, I saw something out of the corner of my eye that stopped me dead in my tracks. It was Ken's four-by-four, zooming across the kitchen floor, heading to the backyard. Pablo was at the wheel.

"Pablo!" I called out, before I could stop my mouth.

"Who's Pablo?" Lanny said, turning around to see who I was talking to.

The four-by-four stopped dead in its tracks. Pablo sat very still, and did his best impression of an action figure. He had done that many times before when one of the sisters caught him driving the halls. The action figure thing worked every time.

"Was that truck there before?" Lanny said. "Funny, I didn't notice it. Not to lecture you, Dan, but you should pick up your toys. Somebody could trip over that."

He shrugged and held out his hand again, which I didn't shake because I was watching Pablo take off and zoom across the kitchen. He drove through the laundry room and out the back door.

Suddenly, Granny Nanny came racing into the kitchen.

"Daniel, can I see you right now?" she said.

"What is it, Granny?"

"I need you to come with me."

"But Lanny and I are in the middle of—"

"That's all right, Dan," Lanny interrupted, standing up and putting on his baseball cap. "You have a lot going on here. I'll go back to the office and draw up some papers. I'll have the contracts sent to your house by the end of the week, so your mom can review them. I know she'll have questions, and I'll be standing by to answer any and all concerns. What do you say?"

"Sounds good," I said.

I didn't even have a chance to say a proper goodbye to Lanny. Granny was practically dragging me by the wrist back to my room. She's strong for an eighty-year-old.

"Look at this," she said, pointing to my computer screen. "It's a message from Pablo."

Lots of times, Pablo writes me notes on my computer. He can type by jumping from one key to another, pouncing on them with all his might. His notes are usually short, because it's really exhausting for him. It's like being on a computer trampoline.

I leaned down and read the message on the screen.

It said:

HEY BRO,

GO AHEAD AND LIVE YOUR LIFE. BE A STAR.
I'M JUST IN THE WAY.

SO LONG. GOT TO FLY, TURKEY PIE.

THE PABS

"What does this mean?" I asked Granny.

"I think he's running away from home," she said.

"Why would he do that?"

"That's a long conversation," Granny said, "which we don't have time for now."

I couldn't believe it. Pablo running away? That was terrible. No, awful. No, the worst thing ever.

"We have to stop him, Granny."

I raced out of my room, through the kitchen, and into the backyard. My eyes scanned the grass, searching for the four-by-four. Finally, I saw it parked over by my mom's office. Maybe I wasn't too late. Maybe he was still there.

I ran to it and looked in the driver's seat, but Pablo was gone.

CHAPTER 13

The Funkster's Funky Fact #13: The average American spends a total of 38.5 days brushing their teeth over a lifetime.

He could have been anywhere in the backyard. When you're as small as a toe and you don't want to be found, it's very easy to stay hidden. The only good thing was that I didn't think he'd had enough time to get very far.

Granny dropped to her hands and knees and started running her hands over the grass near Ken's jeep.

"What was he wearing?" she asked. "I hope it was something bright."

"I don't remember," I told her. "I just saw him for a second this morning. He was mad and wouldn't talk to me."

"I think he was more hurt than mad," Granny said. "It hurt his feelings that you were getting all the attention and he was left out."

"I'm so sorry, Granny. "

"I know you are, hotshot. I just hope you have the chance to tell him that."

I didn't like the sound of that, not one bit.

"We have to find him before he gets too far," she said. "It's a big world out there and Pablo doesn't understand how dangerous it is for him."

While Granny searched the grass, I ran into my mom's office, which is just a few feet away. I thought maybe he might have gone in there. Sometimes Pablo and I would hang out there and play with the animals that were spending the night. In fact, just the night before, we visited an old basset hound named Gus who was recovering from surgery. Pablo really liked him. He said he had a special place in his heart for hound dogs.

Hound dogs! Of course. Now I understood. *You Ain't Nothing but a Hound Dog*, I remembered, and a wave of sadness swept over me.

I had been a real jerk to my brother.

"Gus, have you seen the Pabs?" I whispered to him, sticking my nose up to his cage. He just panted at me, but I had to back away, and fast. His basset hound breath was so bad I thought my nose was going to shrivel up and fall off right then and there.

"Yo, Gus. Ever heard of brushing your teeth?" I said to him. Then I got even sadder because that sounded just like something Pablo would say.

I had to find him.

He wasn't in the office, at least that I could see.
As I turned to go back outside, I bumped smack into
my mom, who was coming in to get the gray gloves.

"Daniel, we're about to begin the hacking process," she said. "It should be exciting to watch."

"Like a hacking cough?" I said. "What's exciting
about that?"

"No, silly. Hacking is what we call the process of releasing a bird of prey into the wild."

"Why'd they give it a name that sounds like a disease?" I said.

She was about to laugh, but suddenly she stopped and looked at me funny. My mom can always tell when there's something wrong.

"What is it, honey? You look so sad."

I wanted to tell her everything. About Pablo. About me. About the secret I'd been keeping for the last month. But all I said was, "I'm okay, Mom."

She nodded. "We'll talk later, Daniel. For now, come see the eagle fly away."

She hurried outside and I just stood there for a minute, thinking about The Pabs. I felt like I was going to cry.

"Got to fly, turkey pie," I muttered.

That was such a strange thing for him to write. Don't get me wrong, he likes to rhyme. But usually his rhymes made sense. This one was just plain silly.

Or was it? Maybe he was telling me something!

Got to fly, turkey pie!

Whoa, my mind went into warp speed. I had a hunch where he was, or at least where he was going! I didn't have a second to lose.

CHAPTER 14

The Funkster's Funky Fact #14: Fingernails grow nearly four times faster than toenails.

Lark and Robin and Goldie were in the backyard, standing around the eagle cage. Lola was next to it, chanting softly. Granny was over by the vegetable garden, frantically checking the undersides of the tomato plant leaves. I knew what she was thinking. Sometimes we get these big green worms there, and Pablo thinks they're cool. Maybe he was hanging out with the tomato worms.

My mom was bending down right at the door of the cage, putting on her thick gloves and talking softly to the bird.

"That's okay, fella. No one's going to hurt you."

As for me, I was on a mission.

I came zooming out of the office like a race car at the finish line. I charged up to Robin who was still holding the can of Diet Coke from the limousine.

"Got to have that, Robs," I said, grabbing it out of her hands and taking a huge swig. I hoped it was still fizzy.

"You are so gross," she said. "Don't backwash in it."

Nothing was happening, so I took another swig, swallowing as much air as I could. Oh yeah, that did it.

I opened my mouth and out came the giccup. The moment I felt it coming, I jumped behind Lola, so no one would see what I knew was about to happen. Almost immediately, I felt the old familiar sensations coming on.

My eyeballs started to growl.

My fingers buzzed and my nose bubbled.

I think Granny heard my knees whistling, because she looked over at me as if to say, *You can't shrink now, hotshot. We have to find Pablo.*

But I did shrink . . . down, down, down, until I was no bigger than a beetle. I was standing in the grass, which now towered above my head like jungle vines. I beat my way through the tall blades, running as fast as I could.

I saw Lola's foot up ahead, which seemed like it belonged to a giant. It was between me and the cage. I wondered if I should go over it or around it. I decided that over it was the shorter route. I jumped onto her little toe and took off running. Then I got the brilliant idea that if I moved to the end of her foot, I could just slide across the bright orange toe-nail polish. I did that, and it was like ice skating. I glided across her toes in no time.

The one thing I hadn't counted on was the swat. My feet must have tickled her, because she reached down to swat me off as though I were a mosquito. She had good aim, and when her fingers hit my back-side, they actually sent me flying. I tumbled through the air and luckily, came in for a landing on the patch of grass right in front of the eagle's cage. I was glad I

was wearing a green T-shirt so no one would spot me. I dropped to my knees, so the grass could cover me, and crawled right up where my mom's sweater was dangling, just above the grass. Then I leapt.

It wasn't an easy jump, but I made it onto the very edge of her sweater. I hung on by my fingernails. I knew she couldn't feel me, because when I'm toe-sized, I'm lighter than a feather. Moving quick as lightning, I started to pump really hard, until I was swinging back and forth. Then, when I was at launch height, I let go and flew through the air, a jump worthy of my best Curtain Crashers move. I nailed the landing, too, ending up smack in the middle of the eagle's tail feathers.

I climbed hand over hand up the big black feather until I reached his wing. By then, my mom was lifting him out of the cage.

"Go home, fella," I heard her say. "Fly safely."

I scurried as fast as I could across his wing, burying my head in his blackish-brown feathers to avoid being seen. Oh no! Those feathers were rubbing against my nose and it was starting to itch. I couldn't allow myself to sneeze. What if I suddenly shot up to my regular size? How would I explain that?

Oh, sorry folks, I was just crawling around in some eagle feathers and I thought I'd pop in for a visit? No, that definitely was not a possibility.

LIN OLIVER

I held my nose and squeezed it as hard as I could. I had to stifle that sneeze. Suddenly, I realized that my whole body was moving up and down. Oh, great. The eagle was flapping his wings, preparing to take off. And yours truly had gotten the wing seat.

Ease up on the flapping action, buddy, I thought to myself. *Give me a minute here to change positions.*

But the bird had realized that he was out of the cage and free, and there was no stopping him. He started to flap his powerful wings faster and faster. I was holding my nose with one hand, and clutching onto his wing with the other.

Here's a tip: If you're ever an inch tall and you find yourself on an eagle who is about to take off, do not hang out on the wing. It can get mighty rough up there. Take it from me. I know what I'm talking about.

As Mr. Eagle beat his wings faster still, I felt like I was on the most humongous roller coaster in the world. First, I'd shoot way way up and then, bamo-slamo, I'd fall way, way down. Way up and way down. Way up and way down. Ugh. My stomach felt like it was in my throat, and not in a good way.

The roller-coaster action made me forget all about the sneezing, that's for sure. It was all I could do to cling on to the wing with both hands. I finally got up the nerve to look down, and sure enough, we were airborne all right. I saw my mom waving good-bye and heard Granny yelling, "Come back! Come back!"

The wind was blowing hard on me from the flapping of his giant wings. It was like being in the middle of a hurricane. I tried as best I could to hold on, but I could feel my fingers slipping. That was definitely not a good thing. Looking down, I saw the ground getting farther and farther away.

Don't let go, Dan, I kept saying to myself.

But my grip wasn't good and I was letting go. I could feel my fingers slipping as we soared higher and higher into the air above Los Angeles.

I held on with all my might, but I just wasn't strong enough.

Look out, ground. Here I come!

LIN OLIVER

The Funkster's Funky Fact #15: Hot dogs originated in Frankfurt, Germany, in 1852. That's why they are also called frankfurters.

I've heard people say that sometimes before people die, they see their whole life flashing in front of them. I'm here to tell you, that's true. As I looked down and saw the city of Los Angeles stretched out before me, a million thoughts raced through my mind. I remembered my dad, the sound of his voice and that hat he wore with a white eagle feather in it. A random picture of my mom flashed through my mind, laughing as she burned the toast like she did at our family breakfasts every Sunday morning. And there was Granny Nanny on her mint green motor scooter and Lola doing some kind of weird tribal dance. You're not going to believe this, but I even saw my sisters, gathered around home plate, waiting to give me a hug when I hit that home run last season against the Mariners.

I felt my fingers slipping and I was sure I was a goner.

We were high up in the sky now, and the eagle's

wings were beating like crazy. I was hanging on by a feather. One more good flap and it was curtains for yours truly, Dan "The Man" Funk.

Suddenly, I looked up and saw a hand reaching out to me. It was just my size, with dirty fingers and chewed-up nails.

"I got you, bro," I heard Pablo say.

So he was on that bird, just like I thought!

Gotta fly, turkey pie.

That was his plan. He wasn't just running away, he was flying away!

"Give me your hand, bro. Now!" he shouted. I could barely hear him what with the wind and all the wing flapping that was going on.

I don't mind telling you, I was afraid to let go. What if he couldn't get me? What if he let go? But I had no choice.

I reached my hand up to him and in a split second, he had it clasped tightly in his. Then he pulled so hard his face turned bright red and the veins on his neck stuck out. With one mighty yank, I was suddenly up next to him, clutching on to a patch of gray feathers right under the eagle's wing. It was plenty windy there, but at least we weren't flapping. We were safe, if only for the moment.

"Thanks, Pabs."

"Don't mention it, bro."

"I'm so sorry about everything."

"Later, dude. I'm a little busy right now. Follow me."

Clutching on to the eagle's feathers, I followed Pablo as we slowly made our way from the wing and onto his chest. The ride was much smoother on his chest, but we were upside-down.

It's a known fact that flying through the air on an

eagle's chest in the upside-down position will make a person highly nauseous. My stomach felt like there were butterflies in there doing somersaults. I know, I know . . . butterflies don't do somersaults, but cut me a break, will you? After all, a person can't get everything right when he's highly nauseous.

"I'm going to ralph," I said to Pablo.

"Not on me, you're not."

"Then I gotta get out of this position."

"Okay, bro. Follow me. I'll try to get you out of here."

Again we climbed across the bird's feathers, heading up this time, across his chest toward his head. His head was easy to see, because it was large and covered with white feathers. As it turns out, bald eagles aren't actually bald, they just look that way because their heads are white. Who knew?

As we crawled up his chest, we got a good look at his beak. We both totally freaked out. When you get a couple minutes to spare sometime, folks, take a look at a picture of a bald eagle and check out the dude's beak. It is big and pointy and sharp and definitely not something you want to mess with. I mean, they can pick up whole rabbits with that thing.

It took us about a nanosecond to decide to take a detour around his beak. Staying as far away from it as we could, we climbed up to his neck, or at least to the part of him that would have been a neck if birds had necks, which I don't think they do.

Finally, after a climb that felt like we were scaling Mount Everest, we arrived on the top of his head. We both plopped down flat on our stomachs to catch our breath. I hung on to his white head feathers with both hands and looked out over the ground below. Pablo did the same.

It was an unbelievable sight. On one side, we could see the waves breaking in the Pacific Ocean. I tried to see if I could locate our house, which is just a few blocks from the beach, but there was no way. We were far too high for that. On the other side, we could see the mountains surrounding Los Angeles, all dotted with pink houses and green leafy trees. And in between the mountains and the sea was the sprawling city of Los Angeles, with its freeways and busy streets and millions of shops and restaurants.

"Look, Pabs," I shouted, pointing down straight under us. "I think I see Pinks."

Pinks is my favorite hot dog stand in the whole world. I probably didn't see it from way up there, but maybe the lack of oxygen was making my brain play funny tricks on me. All I could think about was hot dogs.

"Man, would I love a Pink's chili dog," I said.

"I've never had one," Pablo told me.

"I'll take you there sometime, P. Funk."

"That's a deal, D. Funk."

I would have reached out to high-five him, but at the speed we were going, I wasn't letting go for a second.

We flew in silence after that, except for the flapping of the eagle's wings. I'm telling you, folks. That eagle ride was something I'm never going to forget as long as I live. Flying through the air, so smooth, drifting up and down with the currents—it was total magic. I thought of my mom and dad, and how much they loved birds, and for the first time, I got it. I was proud that my whole name was Daniel *Eagle* Funk, because eagles are strong and graceful, like the one we were riding on. I mean, that bird was one magnificent creature.

Hey, don't worry. I'm not going to become a certifiable bird nut or anything. But I can now officially say I think birds are extremely cool.

At first, Pablo and I were so interested in what we were seeing from up there that we honestly didn't even think about where we were going. After a few minutes, I started thinking about it. Was Mr. Eagle heading south for the winter? Or north for the summer? As far as I knew, we could wind up on a glacier in Alaska or in a jungle in South America. It made me wish that I had listened more to my mom's conversation at the dinner table. When she talked about bird migration, I always took it as a sign for me to tune out and think about baseball statistics.

But I didn't have to wait long to find out where we were going, because it turns out Mr. Eagle had no intention of heading north *or* south. He was heading back to right where he started.

Yup, you got it. The Hollywood sign.

The Funkster's Funky Fact #16: Eagles fly at 20 to 60 miles per hour in normal flight, and dive at up to 120 miles per hour.

There it was, the Hollywood sign, sitting right up on the hill where we had left it the day before. Just seeing it made me think about Lanny Lambert and his offer to make me a star. It was unreal that I had a chance to actually make it big in Hollywood, to be a part of the glamour and fame and other stuff that sign represented.

That eagle definitely had a thing with the Hollywood sign. He kept circling around it, again and again, cocking his head as if he were looking for something down below. I wondered if he really did have a secret desire to make it big in Hollywood. You never know. Maybe he had a hidden talent, like tap dancing or juggling. Don't laugh. It's possible. I mean, who ever thought that I'd be able to shrink to the size of a toe?

Suddenly, the eagle started to flap his wings like crazy and speed up at an incredible rate. I don't know how fast we were going, but it felt like we were blasting off for the moon.

"Hold on tight," I yelled to Pablo. "We're coming in for a landing."

"This totally rocks," he hollered back. "Woo hoo!"

Okay, I admit it. I closed my eyes as we nose-dived down to the ground. I'm up for adventure as much as the next guy, but you try zooming in at over a hundred miles an hour when you're the size of a toe. It makes an airplane coming in for a landing seem like it's going in slow motion.

When I opened my eyes and looked around, we were on the ground in front of one of the huge letters of the Hollywood sign. This time, it wasn't the Y. It was one of the L's. The first one, to be exact.

The eagle made a sound, kind of a combination of a yell and a cackle.

Kleeck-kik-ik-ik-ik, it went.

It sounded pretty loud to my little ears. And then, an amazing thing happened. From behind the first L, there came an answer.

"Kleeck-kaw-ik-kaw-kaw."

Our eagle fluttered along the ground for a few feet until he reached the back of the L. There was another eagle, a little bigger than he was and more brownish in color, sitting on what looked like a big nest of twigs and branches. When the lady eagle saw our guy, she got up off the nest, showing two big eggs right in the middle of it.

"Kleeck-kaw-ik-kaw-ik," she squawked at him. I don't speak Eagle all that well, but I'm pretty sure she was saying, "Your turn to sit on these eggs, Mister. My butt is tired."

I think that's what she said because our eagle headed right over to the nest, sat down on the eggs, and settled in like he belonged there. My mom had told us that in some species of birds, both the male and the female sit on eggs. Judging from what I saw, I figured the eagle was of one of those.

"So that's why he was up here in the first place," I said, turning to Pablo. "He was protecting the nest."

Pablo had already flipped on his back, making a pillow for himself in the soft white feathers of the eagle's head.

"Well, the dude needs to work on his spelling," Pablo said. "Because when we found him, he was at the Y. It's about time he learned the difference between a Y and an L. Even I know that."

"Wait a minute," I said. "Maybe he does know the difference. I'll bet he perched in the Y so no one would notice the nest, over here behind the L. Even Mom didn't notice there was a nest all the way over here."

Pablo gave the eagle's head a little pat.

"You're pretty smart, for a bird," he said.

I flipped onto my back like Pablo, and made a bed just my shape in the white feathers. We were both quiet for a minute. I don't know about Pablo, but I was thinking pretty hard about everything that had gone on between us.

"So what happens now?" I said to him at last. "You coming home?"

"You want me to, bro?"

"More than anything."

"I didn't much like what was happening there," he said.

"I've been thinking about it too," I said to him. "I was a jerk."

"True," he agreed.

"I think I got carried away by the idea of being famous."

"I get it, bro, I really do. It must be exciting to be famous. To be asked to speak in front of all your friends and ride around in limos and have your face plastered all over TV. Who wouldn't want that? It feels good to be seen."

I thought about what he had just said. *It feels good to be seen.*

This time, the little lightbulb went off in *my* little brain. It all became clear. For the first time, I understood what Pablo must have been feeling his whole life. Sure, it's cool to be the size of a toe. No one sees you and you get to do whatever you want. But until I discovered him, only one other person in the whole world knew about Pablo and that was Granny Nanny. Nobody else saw him. He didn't have a family to cheer for him at games. Or a mom to brush the knots out of his hair. Or even a bunch of sisters to make him watch their stupid TV shows with them. He was just plain invisible, and that couldn't feel good.

Suddenly, I knew what I had to do. I sat up straight pushing the feathers aside so I could look right at Pablo.

"You're a great brother," I said to him.

"Wow, where'd that come from, bro?"

"Right here," I said, pointing to my heart.

I know, I know. It was corny. But I always tell you the truth, and the truth is, that's what I said.

"So, are we going home now?" he asked.

"Not right now," I said. "Let's just sit here and wait."

"Wait for what, dude? The Pablo doesn't wait."

"You'll see," I said. "It won't be long now."

LIN OLIVER

The Funkster's Funky Fact #17: The bald eagle holds the record for the largest bird nest ever built. It weighed almost three tons.

Almost an hour went by, but we didn't mind, the Pabs and I. We just hung out there in the soft white feathers of the bald eagle's head. Mr. Eagle seemed pretty cool with that. He was in a much better mood than when he had been in the cage at our house. Why not? His wife was sitting around *kleeck*ing at him and he had two baby eaglets on the way. All in all, life was pretty good up there in the *L*.

Only one thing seemed to annoy him. Every now and then, the transmitter band on his leg would make a little beep and he'd reach down and take a peck at it. Personally, I liked hearing that beep. It meant that my plan was working.

I knew my mom would be tracking the bird. And I knew that when she saw he was back in the Hollywood sign, she was going to come check him out. She'd think he was stuck again or off course. She didn't know about the nest, which was under-standable because she had been looking in the wrong letter. But when she got there and discovered the nest in the *L*, she was going to be one happy bird nut.

After an hour, I heard a car pull up.

"Who's here?" Pablo asked.

"You'll find out soon enough."

I heard the car door slam and then footsteps on the path. It didn't sound like there were a lot of footsteps, just two. One foot for each leg. After a while, I heard her voice.

"Here, fella. Don't be afraid. I won't hurt you."

"It's Mom," Pablo whispered to me. "How'd she get here?"

"She followed the eagle," I said.

"How'd she do that? Is she half bird or something?"

"There's a transmitter band on the eagle's leg," I explained. "Welcome to the wonderful world of modern bird-tracking devices."

The crunching of twigs on the path grew louder as she got nearer. When she reached the Hollywood sign, I could tell that she was looking around the *Y*, where she had found the eagle the first time. Then she must have seen something moving, because she headed over to us, her footsteps thundering in my ears now as she grew closer.

It didn't take her long to spot the nest. An eagle's

nest is no small thing. We're not talking humming-birds here, folks. We're talking three-foot-tall birds who are the size of a small dog.

"A nest," I heard my mom say. "How could I have missed this?"

I think my mom was being a little hard on herself. If you ask me, and I know you didn't, most vets in the world, even the really great ones like my mom, wouldn't think to go looking for an eagle's nest in the Hollywood sign.

Her footsteps were really close now. *Thump, thump, thump.* When I looked up, I could see her hiking boots, and high above them, the big gray gloves.

"Don't be afraid, fella," I heard her say. "Or you either, missy. I just want to check that you're okay."

She was right next to us now, talking softly to the eagle and his wife, making them trust the sound of her voice and the slow, careful movement of her gloved hands. I could feel my heart racing about a million beats a minute. If I was ever going to do this, now was the time. This was my moment, folks.

Was it the right thing to do? Who knows? Right or wrong, I knew it was something I had to do.

I jumped up to my full one-inch height, and waved my arms around like crazy.

"Hey, Mom!" I shouted. "It's me. Here in the feathers!"

She put her face very close to the eagle's head and stared. I looked her right in the eyeball. I could see her eyes grow bigger and bigger until I thought they were going to pop out of her head.

"This must be extremely weird for you, Mom."

"Daniel?" she gasped.

"Yeah, it's me. Listen, Mom. There's something I've been meaning to tell you. I shrink. Not all the time, of course, but enough of the time to make it worth mentioning."

She pulled off her gloves, got down nose-to-nose with me, and poked me with her finger.

"Is it really you?" she whispered.

"In the flesh."

"Oh, my heavens," she just kept saying, over and over again. "Oh, my heavens."

"I'm sorry I didn't tell you about it before, Mom. I should have. It was a really big secret to keep. And there's more to this secret too."

"Oh, my heavens. What more could there be?"

"Be calm, Mom, because this one's even bigger. I mean smaller . . . but in a big kind of way. Oh, why don't I just shut up and show you."

I reached down and grabbed Pablo by the hand and yanked him up to his full upright position. There we were, the two of us toe-sized brothers, standing in

front of our mom for the first time ever.

"Mom, I'd like you to meet your other son, Pablo Picasso Diego Funk," I said.

"Oh, my heavens," she said.

"Yo, Mom!" Pablo flashed her his biggest smile. "I've been waiting to meet you for a long time."

I think you know what she said to that. You got it.

"Oh, my heavens."

She reached out and touched Pablo, running her finger over his little hand, and then his cheek.

"You're real," she said, her voice soft as a whisper.

"The real deal, orange peel," he said.

"Don't mind him," I told her. "He likes to rhyme."

My mom couldn't take her eyes off Pablo.

"Daniel, how long have you known about . . . about him?"

"Not so long. We just met a few weeks ago. We're twins, you know."

"So he was born . . ."

"Yup. In my ear," I said. "It's kind of gross, but that's the way it happened."

She reached out and touched Pablo again, smoothing his hair down the same way she does mine.

"You've been alive, all this time?" she whispered to him.

"Granny said I had to stay a secret," Pablo said. "I

hope you don't get mad and ground me or something, because The Pablo isn't used to being grounded."

"I'm not mad," she said. "I'm happy. So happy to know you exist. Believe it or not, I've always felt your presence."

And then she burst into tears. Not just regular tears, but huge, fat, wet, sloppy tears that fell all over us when she bent down to kiss first his cheek and then mine. Then his cheek, then mine. Then his, then mine. His. Mine. His. Mine.

You get the idea.

"Dude, why is she crying if she's so happy?" Pablo whispered to me in the middle of the kiss fest.

I wanted to tell him that's what girls do. And that they also eat vegetables on their pizza. And wear raspberry-scented lip gloss. And comb one another's hair when it's not even messed up. And end every phone conversation with "love you." I wanted to share with him every single secret I had learned about the Funk women. But I couldn't do a whole lot of talking because we were too busy being smothered by my mom's kisses and covered in her tears of happiness.

And you know what?

It felt really, really good.

CHAPTER 18

The Funkster's Funky Fact #18: In the United States, more pizza is consumed during Super Bowl week than any other week of the year.

ONE WEEK LATER

We were all gathered around the table in the dining room with two large, steaming, delicious pizzas in front of us. Lola had whipped up a batch of stinky tofu for dinner, which is this fermented fried tofu crud she says they lap up in Japan. If that's the case, cancel my ticket to Japan, please.

Everyone but Lola thought her stinky tofu tasted like Stinky Sock Mountain. It was so bad that we took a vote and decided to toss it away and order pizza instead. The vote was seven for pizza and one for stinky tofu. Lola was going to go down fighting.

Now if you're a mathy-sciencey type, you may have learned that seven plus one equals eight, which is a new number for us Funks. It used to be Granny, Lola, Mom, Lark, Robin, Goldie, and me around the dinner table. That makes a total of seven Funks. But now we've added one, and I think you can guess who that is.

Yup, my little brother Pablo.

Now we are eight.

It wasn't easy becoming a family of eight, I'll tell you that. Not that any of my sisters rejected Pablo, or even the idea of a mini-brother. Just the opposite, in fact. It took three days for them to stop fighting over whose room he was going to sleep in and who was going to be in charge of his makeover. Pablo kept insisting that (a) he was going to sleep in my room, and (b) he looked fine the way he was. But they didn't listen, and just went on yapping about how shaggy his hair was and how goofy his clothes were and how sloppy his personal grooming was. To them, Pablo was just a hairdo waiting to happen.

What they *were* freaked out about, however, was my ability to shrink. When I first told them about it, they didn't believe me. They said it was just another one of my made-up stories, like when I told Goldie there was a four-headed snake living under her bed. So I was forced to demonstrate.

After dinner one night I gathered my sisters around the table. I took a giant swig of Coke, let out a huge giccup, and shriveled up to the size of the fourth toe on my left foot, right in front of their eyes.

"Eeuuww," Goldie screamed. "That's disgusting. But cool!"

"And very useful," Lark said. "Daniel, could you crawl inside my computer keyboard and find the pretzel stick that fell in there?"

Robin marched right up to me and said, "If you think that this shrinking thing is going to get you out of clearing the table, then I have some big news for you, little man."

"But Robs, how can I lift a plate that's twenty times my size?" I asked her.

"Well, you're going to have to figure it out fast, Daniel, because we have a chore chart, and last I checked, your name was on it for clearing the table tonight."

"Hey, Robs," I said. "Did you know that when I'm little like this, that pimple on your face looks like a volcano."

"I have a pimple!" she screamed. "No way!"

I knew that would shut her up and get her off the chore topic. Nothing upsets Robin more than a pimple . . . except maybe two pimples.

"Seriously, Daniel, " Lark said, as though she is ever anything but serious. "We need to have rules about shrinking. And Rule Number One should be: No drinking carbonated beverages within a half hour of doing a chore."

"And no shrinking just so you can lie around in my Barbie jacuzzi," Goldie said. "Ken gets jealous."

"And anytime we want, we can ask you to shrink and find stuff that's fallen behind our dressers," Robin said.

"Yeah, even if it's really dusty and gross back there," Goldie added.

Man, oh, man, those Funk women sure know how to suck the fun out of shrinking.

My mom has spent a lot of time getting to know

Pablo and making him special treats like a French fry the size of a pencil point or a Cheerio decorated with strawberry frosting. The Pabs and I were relieved that she wasn't mad at Granny for keeping him a secret.

"She did it out of love," my mom said. "And on the plus side, she did teach him to draw and read. But from now on, he's going to learn math, too. Long division can't be overlooked in a boy's education."

The one thing that's been really hard for my mom to accept is the fact that I shrink. Granny and Pablo and I discussed it and decided that I should try not to do it in front of her for a while.

"GUPs don't take the shrinking deal too well," Pablo said. "I don't see why it's such a biggie for them. But hey, there are a lot of GUP things I don't get, like wearing underwear and covering your mouth when you burp."

Lola loved Pablo right away. As soon as she met him, she invited him into her sweat lodge for a family welcoming ceremony. Poor Pablo totally passed out in there. Lola hadn't realized that when you're the size of a toe, you don't have a lot of extra bodily fluids to spare. We had to lie Pablo down on an ice cube to revive him.

As for the sisters and Pablo, things just got better and better.

Goldie wanted to fix him up on a date with Barbie. We had to explain to her that just because he's little doesn't mean that he wants to go out with an eleven-inch plastic doll.

Robin taught him how to play volleyball using a fake pearl for the ball and a piece of lace on toothpicks for a net. Now he can spike with the best of them.

Lark decided to write a novel about a girl who has a teeny-tiny sister. She was calling it *Little Women* until her English teacher told her that was already the title of a really famous novel. She cried for two days, and then went back to doing her blog instead. Now's she's recording her impressions of what life must be like when you're a toe-sized person. If you're interested, you can check it out on her site I-Have-Nothing-Even-Kind-of-Interesting-to-Say dot com. But as always, don't say I didn't warn you.

As for Pablo, it might surprise you to learn that he is having a lot of fun now that he's officially one of us. He spends a lot of time thinking of ways to drive the sisters nuts, which he says is a total gas. The only problem he has is that now that he's out in the open, he has to take a lot more baths and comb his hair at least once a week. And of course, there's the long-division lessons.

"That's cool, though," he said to me. "The Pablo can manage that. Look what I get in return. A family, dude. That rocks!"

And here's the amazing thing. Now that I officially have a brother in the house, the sisters don't annoy me nearly as much. They spend only half the time picking on me and the other half picking on him. It works out pretty well.

Anyhoo, back to the dining room table. We were just about to dive in and do some serious damage to those pizzas. Pablo was sitting on a little chair Granny made for him out of paper clips and gold leather scraps from one of Robin's old sandals. His place is next to mine, but he sits *on* the table, as opposed to the rest of us, who sit *around* the table.

"Yo, Lark, can you lay a slice of pepperoni on me?" he said, speaking into a little megaphone that my mom had made for him out of a hollowed-out marker cap. He doesn't use it all the time, but when we're all gathered around the dining room table, it helps us all hear him.

"In polite company, the women are supposed to be served first," Lark said.

"Remind me never to be in polite company, then," he hooted.

He held out his hand to me and we high-fived.

Dinnertime had suddenly become fun time when Pablo was there.

I took a slice of pepperoni for myself and tore off a smidgen for him. It was about the size of a pencil eraser. He gobbled it up like he hadn't eaten for a month. I'd noticed that since he had joined in family meals, he was eating a lot. I think he liked being with all of us at the table. It sure beat eating all alone in Granny's room.

"This is gooey, just the way I like it," he said, sucking down a long, messy strand of cheese.

"Eeuuww," Robin said. "You talk with your mouth full, just like Daniel."

"And your problem with that is what?" he slurped.

We both cracked up again and held up our hands to high-five. Then he reached down and wiped some tomato sauce off his mouth with his cape.

"Gross," said Goldie. "Barbie doesn't like boys who don't have good manners."

"Well, Golds, you tell Barbie that I personally saw Ken blowing his nose in his hand."

I laughed so hard that a piece of pizza actually went up my nose and came out my left nostril.

Man, oh, man, it was good having a brother in the house.

Just then, the phone rang.

"Not getting it," I said.

"It's probably for me anyway." Robin jumped from the table and ran to the living room phone.

"Robin's residence," she said. "Speak only if you're cute."

Then she burst into a spontaneous giggle fit.

Pablo and I shot each other a look. Girls. They're either laughing for no reason or crying for no reason. Not like us guys who can just kick back and enjoy some wrestling on TV with nothing but a bag of pretzels to keep us happy.

"Oh, hi," Robin said into the phone. "Just a minute, I'll tell him."

She came leaping over to the table, sticking the phone in my face.

"It's him," she said. "Lanny Lambert. He says he's got your offer all ready and wants to send the papers over."

I looked over at Pablo. He stood up, walked over to my plate and leaned against my glass of milk.

"Go ahead, bro. You can say yes. I'm cool with that."

I took the phone from Robin.

"Hello, Mr. Lambert," I said. "This is Daniel. I'm fine, thank you. Really good, in fact."

Granny Nanny waved her hand at me to get my attention.

"I know you'll do the right thing, hotshot," she whispered.

I cleared my throat and spoke into the phone. "Mr. Lambert," I said. "I want to tell you that I've changed my mind. I don't really want to be a star and we're not going to sign your papers."

"Dude," Pablo said. "You don't have to do that."

"No, really, Mr. Lambert," I said. "I've thought about it a lot. And what I think is this."

I looked at Pablo, who had left the milk glass and walked across my pepperoni pizza to stand right in front of me.

"Maybe sometime I'll want to take you up on your offer, because it's very cool to be seen by a whole lot of people," I said. "But right now, I'm very happy where I am. As a matter of fact, I have everything I want right here."

I snapped the phone shut.

"Bro, I'm crying here," Pablo said.

He put his hand out and we were just about to high-five. But before we could make contact, we were surrounded by all six of the Funk women— well, seven if you count our bulldog, Princess. They all threw their arms around me and The Pabs, laughing and crying all at once. I could barely breathe, and Pablo was almost squished like a fly.

There we were again, with the Funk women blithering all over us.

If you ask me, and I know you didn't, a group hug with your sisters can be pretty darn fun.

Just don't tell anyone I said that, okay?

EPILOGUE

Hey, guys. It's me, The Pablo.

Daniel thinks he's the man because he writes all those prologues and everything.

Well, check this baby out. It's called an epilogue.

That's right. It's like a prologue except it comes at the end instead of the beginning of a book.

And I, The Pablo, am writing it.

The problem is, I don't have much time. I promised my brother and sisters that I'd play mini golf with them.

And when I say mini, I'm not kidding.

In fact, I hear them calling now.

Got to jet, Brett.

And until we meet again, do your thing, chicken wing.

Love,

The Pabs